THE
GENESIS FILES

THE GENESIS FILES

GWEN RICHARDSON

Cushcity Communications
www.gwenrichardson.com

Cushcity Communications
14300 Cornerstone Village Dr., Suite 370
Houston, TX 77014

The Genesis Files   Copyright © 2012 Gwen Richardson

ISBN- 13:   978-0-9800250-8-8
ISBN- 10:   0-9800250-8-7

First Printing June 2012
Printed in the United States of America

10 9 8 7 6 5 4 3 2 1

This is a work of fiction. Any references or similarities to actual events, real people, living or dead, or to real commercial enterprises are intended to give the novel a sense of reality. Any similarity in other names, characters, places and incidents is entirely coincidental.

Distributed by Cushcity Communications
Submit Wholesale Orders to:
Cushcity.com
Attn: Order Processing
14300 Cornerstone Village Dr., Suite 370
Houston, TX 77014
Phone: 1-800-340-5454
Fax: (281) 583-9534

DEDICATION

To my younger brother, Dr. Linwood Daye Jr., who passed away Dec. 23, 2007, long before I ever anticipated losing a sibling. A year before he died, I told him I was going to write this book.
He is forever in my thoughts.

CHAPTER 1

"Lloyd, are you okay in there?" Stephanie called to him from the bedroom. "I don't hear any water running either in the sink or the toilet." She paused, listening for a response. "What are you doing?"

"Nothing. My stomach was feeling a little queasy and I came in here just in case, but I'm fine now," Lloyd replied from the bathroom, knowing he wasn't telling his wife the truth. But what difference did it make? Stephanie couldn't solve this problem and there was no need to worry her with it.

Lloyd Palmer was not looking forward to another frustrating day as a reporter for the *Houston Ledger*. When the alarm clock buzzed that morning, he hit the snooze button for the third time. He lay in bed thinking about how fed up he was after ten years working at a dead-end job, for an editor who Lloyd was certain spent his weekends with members of the local KKK klavern.

Stephanie had been lying beside him snoring lightly. He had contemplated waking her up for a quick lovemaking session before heading to the office. He'd had trouble relaxing the night before and wanted to wake her up when he got into bed after midnight, but Stephanie had been sleeping so soundly that he decided not to. Now he was in the bathroom dreading the impending day at work.

He'd had high hopes for his career when he graduated from the University of Missouri with a degree in journalism. There were only a handful of blacks there who shared his major, his love for observing events and writing about them. The recruiters all told him he had his pick of journalism positions and could work in virtually any city.

Lloyd decided to go the small town route—get experience at a limited circulation newspaper to learn the ropes of the business. He spent two years at the daily paper in North Little Rock, Arkansas, then moved to Petersburg, Va., for another five years at the *Daily Reporter*.

Stephanie, who had been his high school sweetheart, made his stints in both cities bearable. But the small town atmosphere didn't suit him; he needed a little more culture, a little more night life, a little more pizzazz.

About a year before he moved to Houston, he'd broken an important story while in Virginia. A state senator was caught taking bribes from corporate bigwigs and Lloyd's inside sources had been instrumental in feeding him crucial, salacious details. The story made national headlines and, as a result, Lloyd was thrust into the national spotlight and interviewed on several cable television news programs.

When he received a call from the *Houston Ledger* to take a job as a beat reporter with promises of moving up the journalistic ladder, he jumped at the chance. The *Ledger* was the city's daily newspaper and had the largest circulation in the state of Texas.

As a schoolteacher, Stephanie had always been able to find work wherever they moved. Their daughter, Bria, was just entering first grade then, so the time was right to put down roots in a major city without disrupting her education.

Little did Lloyd know there wasn't going to be much room for advancement. In order for him to get promoted, some of the old heads had to move on, retire or find jobs in other locales.

With subscribers rapidly going to the Internet for their news and newspaper circulation dropping like a rock, everybody was afraid to take a risk. The old boys were waiting to retire and collect on their 401(k)s, meaning there wasn't a snowball's chance in Hades that Lloyd would move up.

Ed Jackson, Lloyd's boss, had been at the *Ledger* literally his entire career, and was among those unlikely to retire any time soon. During his reign as editor, not a single black reporter had ever been promoted even though more than two dozen had worked in the newsroom. And when black employees said, "Good morning" to Ed, he barely acknowledged their existence unless it was absolutely necessary.

According to Ed, Lloyd's story ideas were either not current enough, not relevant enough or not mainstream enough to be of interest to the *Ledger* readership. "Just do what I tell you to do and don't ask any questions," Ed had said to him yesterday when Lloyd had pitched an idea for a story about a charter school in a low-income area whose students were scoring in the top percentile on state achievement tests. Lloyd despised Ed more and more every day.

At age forty-five, Lloyd should have been at the pinnacle of his career, not stuck in a dead end job with a boss he could barely stomach. Something had to give.

Since he was a little boy, Lloyd had been a star in everything he'd done. He was always at or near the top of his class, a star athlete and well-liked. He was supposed to make a difference. His parents, who lived in Navasota, Texas, had been so proud of him when he graduated from college—the first in his family to go to the next level educationally.

His mother, Rochelle, had been a domestic most of her life, spending her last ten working years making beds and cleaning toilets for a hotel chain. His father, Allen, an assembly line worker, spent thirty years with the same company, but foreign competition forced the older, higher-waged employees into early retirement.

Allen spent most of his days now relaxing and working in the garden, while his wife, Rochelle, kept house and crocheted. Both of his parents came from a long line of proud, God-fearing people who wanted a better life for their children.

All of these thoughts were going through Lloyd's mind as he stared in the mirror. His reflection spoke to him: he was still handsome and in relatively good physical shape. Women still flirted with him. He'd even had a few, like Audrey Moore, go beyond flirting to practically accosting him in the break room at work.

"When are you going to ask me for my digits?" Audrey had whispered in his ear yesterday as he was fixing his morning cup of coffee. She practically put her tongue in his ear as she whispered, and he maneuvered his way around her to go to his desk.

"I told you, Audrey. There's only one woman for me," he'd said. But taking hints was not one of Audrey's strengths.

His frustration was not with the way he looked; he was reasonably secure with that. He just couldn't get over the feeling that he was wasting time, treading water until some cause that was both meaningful and massive entered his life.

Of course, Stephanie knew about the pressures he was experiencing at work, but she always reminded him that, in the current economy, he was lucky to have a secure job with good benefits. With their high mortgage, car notes, credit card debt and Bria's impending college years, he couldn't afford to make waves. They'd need every penny they'd invested in her college fund to pay her tuition to a decent school.

No, he was going to have to stick it out at the *Ledger*, for now. Maybe things would get better for him at work soon. They couldn't get much worse.

CHAPTER 2

Lloyd was grooving to the sounds of the rhythm and blues crooner Maxwell while he headed to the *Ledger* headquarters on the I-45 freeway. Traffic was bumper-to-bumper as usual, but not bad for a Friday morning.

He pulled into the underground parking garage and saw his co-worker and friend, Charles Scott, heading toward the elevator. With his blonde, all-American good looks, Charles was easy to like—especially for the ladies. He was single, always juggling at least two or three girlfriends, and drank too much. But he was a damn good reporter. Lloyd got out of his car and ran to catch up with him.

"Hey man, have you heard anything popping this morning?" asked Lloyd. Charles had a nose for the latest gossip and had lots of sources feeding him information.

"Not much so far, but the day is young."

They both got off the elevator and headed to the news room. The office was humming. Reporters and their aides were already busy checking the Internet for news from the major newspapers, wire services, blogs and the morning talk shows. Just then, Lloyd saw Audrey Moore heading his way. The woman wore too much makeup, showed too much cleavage, and was always hinting, in a not-so-subtle way, that she couldn't wait to get busy with him.

"Hi, Lloyd," she said, using her most seductive voice. "What did *you* do last night?"

"Hi, Audrey. My wife and I spent a quiet evening at home." Lloyd constantly reminded Audrey of the fact that he was married, but it didn't seem to matter to her. If she wasn't one of the most efficient office assistants the *Ledger* had ever had, he might report her behavior and get her fired. But Lloyd didn't want the hassle of her potentially turning the tables on him and claiming that he had sexually harassed her.

She wasn't his type, even if he had been a single man. Lloyd liked to take charge in a relationship, at least at the beginning.

"Well, don't forget what I told you," she whispered as she came closer to him. "If you ever need some excitement, I'm available most evenings."

"I'm not looking for any excitement," said Lloyd. "But if I think of any guys who may be looking for a date, I'll let you know." He'd tried everything to discourage her, but nothing seemed to work.

Lloyd went to his desk and checked his e-mail. He often picked up some of his best leads through anonymous e-mail communications. He scrolled down and checked the stuff that had come in overnight. Nothing even remotely interesting.

Just as he was finishing up, he saw Ed walking in his direction at a quickened pace. At age sixty, Ed was completely bald and always seemed to be sweating, even when it was cold outside. If Ed was coming to see him this early in the morning, it could mean only one thing, some overnight murder or something just as depressing. Lloyd braced himself.

"Lloyd, I have a hot story I'd like you to cover."

"What's up, Ed?"

"There's been a murder-suicide in a high-rise apartment complex in the Galleria area," he said. "An executive from one of the oil companies caught his fianceé in bed with another guy. He offed both of them and then turned the gun on himself. There may be more to the story, so I want you to cover all of the angles."

"Sounds pretty open and shut to me," said Lloyd. "Can't you give this to someone else? I've been working on a story about the new legislation in the state Senate that could create some new charter schools in Third Ward . . ."

"No," Ed barked. "The story on the legislation can wait. You know how the Senate is — they could debate the issue for a whole year and then do nothing. This story can get you a byline on the front page, and that's what you've been asking for lately, isn't it?"

"Well, you have a point there," said Lloyd as he acquiesced. "What are the victims' names and what's the address?"

"Everything's here," said Ed, as he handed Lloyd a printout of the basic information about the victims. "The police have already taped off the area, and the Forensics Department is there now. I want you to do the usual—talk to the police, interview the neighbors, see if anyone has heard them arguing, throwing things . . . ."

"I get the picture," said Lloyd, as he began packing up his note pad, digital voice recorder and laptop for the thirty-minute drive to the Galleria. "What's my deadline?"

"Send me something with the basic facts as soon as possible, by two o'clock this afternoon, so we can get it uploaded on the web site," said Ed. "You can send revisions as you conduct the interviews and gather more facts. Get moving."

Lloyd walked briskly out of the office to the garage, got in his car, and headed toward the Galleria. When he got close to the high-rise apartment where the crime took place, there were multiple sheriffs' vehicles and a station wagon from the Harris County Coroner's Office. He parked, walked toward the entrance and showed his media credentials to the sheriff. Then he took the elevator to the fifteenth floor. When he got off the elevator, there were at least ten cops who were collecting evidence, taking statements from other tenants on the floor or communicating on two-way radios.

Lloyd approached the sheriff in front of apartment 1504, where the shooting had occurred. "Can you point out the officer in charge?" Lloyd asked.

"That would be Sheriff Arnold over there," said the officer, as he pointed to a tall, dark-haired, heavy-set man wearing sunglasses.

"Thanks," said Lloyd and he walked over to Sheriff Arnold with his pad and digital recorder. The victims were covered with sheets, but Lloyd could still see their limbs sticking out from underneath and blood-soaked carpet around the bodies.

There was blood on the walls and on the lamp shade that had been knocked to the floor. There were bullet holes in the walls too, and it looked like there may have been a struggle before the shooting.

"Sheriff Arnold, may I ask you a few questions about the crime scene?" Lloyd asked as he flashed his media credentials.

"Sure. We have a forty-year-old white male, identified as Henry Banks, shot at close range with a 32-caliber weapon from what appears to be a self-inflicted wound," said Arnold. "Another white male, identified as Joseph Frank, was also shot at close range with the same weapon, with multiple gunshot wounds. A thirty-five-year-old white female, Laurie Doolittle, has a gunshot wound to the head."

"Time of death appears to be approximately 2:00 o'clock this morning. The next of kin have been notified."

"Was there a suicide note found anywhere?" asked Lloyd.

"No, but one of the neighbors reports hearing loud voices—what sounded like an argument—before hearing several gunshots in succession. The nature of the argument is unknown at this time, but from the looks of it, this was a lovers' quarrel," continued Arnold, as he made some notes on a police report form attached to a clipboard.

"Do you know which oil company Banks worked for?"

"ExTron Oil and Gas. He was one of the top executives there. Apparently, he had an ex-wife and two kids but, except for child support payments, he's been estranged from them for a number of years," added Arnold.

"Anything else I should know about?"

"This was definitely a crime of passion," said Arnold, "since Banks shot his fiancee's lover at least ten times, which means he had to reload his weapon. I guess he saved the last few bullets for himself."

"I'll go make my rounds now among the neighbors and see what else I can find out about him," said Lloyd. "I may have a few more questions for you before I leave."

"I'll be here another hour or so," said Arnold.

Lloyd exited the apartment and decided to get started right away interviewing neighbors while the facts were fresh in their minds. He knocked on the door of the apartment immediately across the hall and waited for a response. No one answered.

He then knocked on the door adjacent to Banks' apartment. He thought he heard a television playing and movement inside. A woman's voice asked, "Who is it?"

"I'm Lloyd Palmer with the *Houston Ledger*. I'd like to ask you a few questions about your next door neighbor, Henry Banks."

"Okay," the woman replied, and Lloyd could hear her unlatching the chain on the door. Everybody wanted their fifteen minutes of fame. People liked getting their names in the paper, unless there was a possibility of retaliation from someone involved with the crime. In this case, the perpetrator was dead.

An attractive, red-haired woman in her mid-thirties opened the door. She had on a silk robe, but no makeup. The scent of her perfume was overwhelming. "How can I help you?" she said.

"Did you know about the shooting next door?" asked Lloyd.

"Yes. I woke up about 2:00 a.m. to what sounded like gunshots. I was sound asleep when it happened; but the noise woke me up, and I heard several gunshots after that. I called 911," she said.

"Did you know Mr. Banks?"

"I only knew him in passing. I'd mostly speak to him coming and going. Sometimes I'd see him and his girlfriend coming in late at night, but he and I never had a real conversation about anything," she said.

"Ever overhear any of their conversations?" asked Lloyd.

"About a week ago, I heard loud voices coming from the apartment that sounded like the two of them having an argument," she said. "But I couldn't make out exactly what they were saying."

"How long would you say the argument lasted?"

"Well, I wasn't timing it or anything, but it lasted for several minutes. Afterwards, his girlfriend slammed the door and stormed out. I looked through my peephole and saw her leaving. I haven't heard anything else since then, until this morning."

"I see. May I have your name and phone number, please, in case I need to contact you again about any more details?" asked Lloyd.

Lloyd jotted down the number and the woman's name, Glenda Krantz. "Here's my card in case you remember something in the meantime."

Krantz looked at the card, nodded and closed the door. She basically confirmed what Sheriff Arnold had told him, but Lloyd thought she might remember something later.

Lloyd then knocked on the apartment next to hers. He paused for a moment to see if anyone was home. He thought he heard some chanting or meditating and put his ear to the door.

He knocked again—louder, this time. The chanting stopped and he heard footsteps approaching. The door opened slowly, and a tall, very dark-skinned man peered out. The chain was still latched on the door.

"Yes, may I help you?" the dark-skinned man said. He appeared to be in his sixties and had an accent—Lloyd was certain it was African, but couldn't identify the region. On his head was an off-white yarmulke, the traditional head covering for Jewish males.

"My name is Lloyd Palmer and I'm with the *Houston Ledger*. I'd like to ask you a few questions."

"What about, my son?" he said. Lloyd was intrigued by the man's use of such an endearing term for a stranger. He also noticed the man was wearing some garb Lloyd had never seen before.

"Your neighbor down the hall was involved in a murder-suicide early this morning. I'm questioning some of the people on this floor to see if they heard anything or saw anything last night that might shed some light on the crime," said Lloyd.

"My son, I do not concern myself with such matters. I did not know this man, and I keep to myself, which is the custom of our people," said the African.

"Where are you from, if I may ask?" queried Lloyd, hoping the man would open up and reveal more about himself.

"Zimbabwe, a country in southern Africa. Perhaps you have heard of it."

"Of course, I have. And what is your name?" Lloyd probed further.

"Excuse me if I insulted you; it was unintentional," the African replied. "But I find that most Americans, particularly those who are black, know very little about Africa. They seem to think of the continent as one country."

"My name is Rudo Hamisi. But I do not want my name in your newspaper. People whose names appear in your newspaper always seem to meet with misfortune, either before or after their names are printed."

"We only print the facts, stories about what actually happened," said Lloyd, who felt like he needed to defend his profession.

"And how do you determine which stories appear in your newspaper?" asked Hamisi. "The themes seem to be death, disaster, and destruction. Is that really all that is newsworthy on an average day in America?"

Deep down, Lloyd knew Hamisi was right but was somewhat irritated that he was being so judgmental. "That is what people are most interested in," replied Lloyd defensively.

He then noticed the peculiar markings on the shawl Hamisi had around his shoulders. One of the markings appeared to be the image of an elephant inside the Star of David. "We can't sell newspapers if we print a bunch of stories that nobody wants to read."

"So your job is to tell people what they want to hear in order to make money. You do not tell them what they need to know?" asked Hamisi.

Lloyd could sense the sarcasm in Hamisi's question, but he did not have a good answer. He checked his watch. He needed to file the first installment of the story soon.

"Mr. Hamisi, that is an over-simplification of what we do. But I'm on a deadline and need to file my story concerning your neighbor's suicide in a couple of hours. I may need to contact you later to follow up in case you remember something. Would it be okay to call you or stop by later?" asked Lloyd, who doubted that Hamisi had anything to add to the story, but there was something about him that piqued Lloyd's curiosity.

"As I said, I do not wish for my name to appear in your newspaper," responded Hamisi. "But if I can be of help to you, you may come by."

"Here's my card," said Lloyd, and handed it to Hamisi. "My home phone number is on the back."

Hamisi did not offer a phone number, and Lloyd did not ask. It was as if the African was giving Lloyd an invitation to visit again—not to enlighten him with titillating details about the unfortunate Mr. Banks, but to share some wisdom, some knowledge that Lloyd needed to receive. There was a spiritual connection between them; Lloyd could feel it. He knew he'd be back—Hamisi's aura compelled him.

CHAPTER 3

Lloyd had a source in the homicide department at the Harris County Sheriff's Office, and he decided to call her. The law enforcement officers had confiscated Banks' laptop and the hard drive to his computer at work, and Lloyd wondered if any incriminating e-mails had been found. If he could get some inside information from his source, that would make the completion of his story a lot easier.

He found her phone number among his cell phone contacts and selected it. She picked up on the first ring.

"Sheriff's Office, Karen Taylor speaking," she said.

"Karen, this is Lloyd Palmer at the *Houston Ledger*. How are you?"

"I'm doing great, Lloyd. But I know you didn't call me to chit-chat." Karen got straight to the point. "What do you want?"

"Have you seen anything come across your desk regarding the Henry Banks murder-suicide case?" Lloyd asked.

"They've catalogued his e-mails and a history of web sites he visited. It appears that he intercepted some of his fiancée's e-mails from her lover. Some of it was pretty graphic stuff. The guy she was seeing even e-mailed her some nude photos of his, uh, male equipment, if you get my drift."

"It must have been enough to send Banks over the edge. The crime scene was pretty gruesome," said Lloyd. "Is there any way you can send me a copy of those e-mails?"

"No way. Management periodically monitors our e-mails and Web traffic and I'm not going to get fired for leaking information to you. I've told you more than I should have already."

"Well, can you print out a few of the e-mails and meet me later this afternoon?" pleaded Lloyd. "That way, there won't be an e-mail trail."

Karen knew she had helped Lloyd in the past, but she wanted to make him sweat a little. "What's in it for me?"

"I'll give you a hundred bucks," Lloyd responded. The newspaper had a petty cash fund specifically for this purpose, although it was never documented as such on any formal expense report. It was classified as "market research."

"Okay. Meet me in thirty minutes in the Best Buy parking lot on Richmond Avenue near the Galleria. Can you do that?" asked Karen.

"I'll be there. I'll be driving a black Toyota Camry," said Lloyd. Depending on the content of the e-mails, their inclusion in the story, along with the facts that Lloyd had already gathered, should be more than enough to file his first installment, just in time for the deadline.

Lloyd got in his car and headed toward Richmond Avenue. He got to the parking lot within ten minutes — but he'd rather be early than late. He didn't want to miss Karen. While he was waiting, he opened his laptop and began to work on the story. He used the working headline, "ExTron Executive Killed in Murder-Suicide," but he knew that Ed was likely to change whatever he submitted.

He then began with the lead sentence and the facts about the story, leaving room to fill in details contained within the e-mails Karen would be giving him. A few minutes later, he looked up and saw Karen's car slowly passing by. He waved at her and she pulled her car alongside his. Lloyd handed her the $100 bill, and Karen gave him several sheets of paper. She drove away quickly — no need to linger and take a chance that someone she knew would see her.

Lloyd looked through the e-mails. Karen had given him lots of material; she even printed out a color image of the photograph she mentioned. Banks' fiancée was messing around with a pretty weird guy. He'd sent several photos of his private parts from different angles, inserting arrows and lewd remarks on the side. Pretty sordid stuff, but juicy material for his story.

Lloyd's journalistic counterparts from the 1960s had covered history-making events: Ground-breaking school desegregation cases, sit-ins at lunch counters, freedom rides across the South, civil rights marches, the assassinations of historical icons. Forty years later he, on the other hand, was relegated to reporting what, in many cases, could be classified as soft porn.

Lloyd was then reminded of Hamisi and the things he had said about what was printed in the newspaper. Lloyd knew this was sleazy material, not worthy of someone like him who was supposed to accomplish something of substance, but that was what was expected of him as a reporter. He had to put that out of his mind, for now.

He called ExTron's Public Affairs Department and spoke to the young lady who answered. She provided him with Banks' personal information: job title, number of years with the company, countries where he'd worked, and the names of his ex-wife and children.

Lloyd put the finishing touches on his story and forwarded it to his editor. He'd follow up with the sheriff's office just in case more details came in, but his work for today was essentially done.

He opened his cell phone and called Ed to see what he thought of the story. "Hi, Ed. It's Lloyd. I just sent you the Banks murder-suicide story."

"I'm reading it over now, Lloyd," said Ed. "Excellent work. You've got some really good stuff and the information in the e-mails was priceless. This story will definitely make the front page with your byline. If you get any new material that we need to add or revise, let me know right away. We can always upload the revised version to the web site. Otherwise, feel free to go on home. Frankly, Lloyd, this was a lot more than I had hoped for. I didn't know you had it in you."

Lloyd shuddered at Ed's insult. Ed always had a way of turning what should have been a compliment into something condescending.

Lloyd should have been happy about the front-page exposure, but his triumph was bittersweet. As he got on the 610 Loop and headed home for a weekend of rest and relaxation, he thought about his parents and was glad they didn't read the *Ledger* every day. They still had high hopes that Lloyd's reporting would end up in history books or win him one of the top journalism awards. This was one story he'd written that he hoped they'd miss.

CHAPTER 4

Lloyd pulled into the driveway of his home in Northwest Houston and breathed a sigh of relief. He'd beat most of the rush-hour traffic and was glad to see that Stephanie's car was in the driveway.

Even though they had been married almost twenty years, Stephanie still brought out the passion in him. Sure, she'd put on a few pounds, but so had he. She had a way of making him chase her without making him beg. Sometimes he would be at work, think about her, and his nature would rise right there in the office.

As he entered his home, he heard his wife in the kitchen preparing food for the evening. "Steph, I'm home," he yelled, so she could hear him above the sounds of cabinets closing and pots banging.

"You're home early," Stephanie replied. "Everything go okay at work?"

"Yes, I covered a story in the Galleria area, but I was able to wrap things up around three-thirty. Ed said it was okay for me to head for home, as long as I checked in to update any new info that may come in about the story. I need to check again before dinner, just in case."

Lloyd placed his laptop on the kitchen table, checked for additional e-mails and browsed the Internet for news reports. He went to the *Ledger's* web site and, sure enough, the home page already had his story front and center, with photos of Banks, his fianceé and her lover, as well as the front of the apartment building where the murder-suicide took place. Lloyd decided he would tell Stephanie about it later. He wanted to unwind before their guests arrived later that evening.

One Friday each month, the Palmers and their friends, Ron and Shirley Singleton, got together for dinner and a game of cards, and tonight was their night to be the hosts. Lloyd and Ron had been best friends since college and loved to play spades.

Ron was a structural engineer for the City of Houston. The Singletons' daughter, Destiny, was one of Bria's close friends, so the teenagers would often go to a movie or the mall while the adults played cards. They usually arrived around seven o'clock so Lloyd had a couple of hours to relax.

Lloyd went into the den, sat in his recliner and put on his headphones as he listened to smooth jazz. He thought a lot about the events of the day, especially Hamisi and the things he had said. Lloyd had a strange feeling that fate had brought the two of them together.

One question that Hamisi asked Lloyd kept sticking in his mind: "You do not tell them what they need to know?" As a reporter, Lloyd always believed that's what he was doing. Now he wasn't so sure.

Lloyd needed his life to have more purpose than just reporting the latest episodes of death and destruction to the masses. He was sick of crime scenes and fatal traffic accidents with bodies strewn on the freeway. He was tired of drug shootouts, child abuse cases and government corruption and ineptitude. He was frustrated that, for the black community, the media seemed to be mostly interested in covering situations which proved the negative premise: Black people were either too stupid or too brutal to succeed.

Lloyd put his head back, relaxed and finally dozed off. The ringing of the doorbell woke him up a couple of hours later. Stephanie answered the door and Ron and Shirley walked in with their hands laden with food containers. Destiny came in behind them and ran upstairs to Bria's room.

"Hey, everybody," said Shirley. "Are you and Ron ready to get whooped again tonight?" she said, referring to Lloyd and Ron being spades partners. She and Stephanie had beaten them badly during their last Friday night session. They always played with the ladies versus the men; the ladies won most of the time.

"Y'all just got lucky last time," said Ron. "But me and my partner are going to put a hurting on you this week."

Ron helped Shirley carry the items into the kitchen and then headed to the den as Lloyd was making an effort to look like he hadn't just spent two hours sleeping.

"What's up, man?" asked Ron, as he sat down on the sofa.

"Nothing much," replied Lloyd. "Just finished writing a story on the murder-suicide near the Galleria. Did you hear about it?"

"I heard something on the radio on the way over here, but not too many details. It seems there is at least one murder in Houston every day of the week," said Ron.

"Well, the guy really went on a rampage. Some people can't handle being cheated on by someone they love," said Lloyd.

"You're right about that," Ron said. "But if I caught Shirley cheating, the last thing I'd do is kill myself. I love my wife, but I have a daughter to think of. And my attitude is: I don't want anybody who doesn't want me."

"Sho' nuff, man." Then Lloyd said, "I want to talk to you about something else—about my job. Dealing with so much negativity day after day is taking its toll. I'm fed up with seeing dead bodies. I might look for another job or even another profession."

"What are you talking about, Lloyd? I thought you loved being a reporter."

"My concept of being a journalist is a lot different from what I actually do on a daily basis. When I was in college, I thought I would be writing about major events, sweeping legislation, things like that. Instead, it seems that as the years go by, my work carries me deeper and deeper into the gutter," said Lloyd.

"And I don't know if my boss can be any more patronizing than he's been for the last ten years. Any hope I might have had of a major career move isn't going to happen as long as Ed is my supervisor. The guy thinks I'm an idiot. Plus, he's a racist."

"He can't be that bad," said Ron. "You know how hard it is to find a job these days, and unemployment checks aren't enough to cover your mortgage and car note, let alone Bria's college fund."

"Don't remind me because that's exactly what Steph says when I even try to broach the subject. I'm just not sure I can go through this life with nothing more to show for my existence than a scrapbook filled with murder clippings. I used to talk to my parents about some of the stories I would write, but now I mostly hope they don't ask any questions. That way, I don't have to go into the details and see the disappointed looks on their faces."

"But I don't want to waste your time listening to me wallow in self pity. How's your job going?" asked Lloyd.

"Well, I think all of us may have had unrealistic expectations in college. We all thought we were going to change the world and, instead, the world changed us," said Ron. "I enjoy engineering and I get a sense of gratification when a project is completed. But it does get monotonous at times."

"Something interesting did happen to me today," said Lloyd. "I met an unusual man when I was questioning folks at the crime scene of the murder-suicide. He's from Africa — Zimbabwe, he said — and he seems to be some sort of religious tribal leader. Meeting him was one of the most fascinating encounters I've had in a long time."

"Oh, yeah? What made it so fascinating?"

"First of all, he was wearing clothes that I haven't seen before. And, instead of me asking him questions, he was questioning me in ways that I had never thought of before," said Lloyd.

"Maybe you can learn more about him. There might be a story there somewhere."

"Are you kidding? For one thing, Mr. Hamisi — that's the man's name — said he didn't want his name to appear in our newspaper. He acted as if it was a bad omen or something and essentially told me that people whose names appear in our paper have bad luck," said Lloyd. "The funny thing is that I really couldn't disagree with him on that point."

"Besides, Ed only wants pictures of two types of black people in the *Ledger* — victims or perpetrators. He's never actually come out and said it, but actions speak louder than words. Ninety percent of the photos of black people who appear in the paper fall within those two categories."

"Well, Ed may be a cretin, but he still wants to sell newspapers. If there's a story about Hamisi or his people that could create a buzz among the readership, I'd bet Ed would go for it."

"If I pitch him the idea, he'll just shoot it down, like he has every other story I've suggested."

"Maybe you should write the story first, and then present it to him. Do the background and research in your spare time so Ed won't know about it. After he looks it over, even if he refuses to publish the story, can't you pitch it to some other publications?" asked Ron.

Lloyd was skeptical. "I don't know, man. Sounds like a waste of time to me."

"What do you have to lose? At the very least you may uncover a compelling topic and, if the story doesn't appear in the *Ledger*, it might get published somewhere else. Letting Ed know that you have other options may even make you more valuable to him," said Ron.

"Remember some of the girls we used to like in college?" Ron continued. "Sometimes they didn't notice us until some other girl took an interest. Ed could be the same way. Once he sees that another newspaper or magazine likes your work, you'll gain his respect."

"You could be on to something. I'll give it some thought," Lloyd said, as they both heard Stephanie calling them for dinner.

"We'd better go eat," said Ron. "We need our energy to win the spades game tonight. The last thing I want to hear in the car on the way home is Shirley's mouth, bragging about how she and Steph ran another Boston on us."

"I hear you," said Lloyd, as they walked together toward the kitchen.

CHAPTER 5

Days like this one made Lloyd hate being a reporter. It was Monday morning and, as soon as Lloyd woke up, Ed called him about a car chase and a shooting. The victim was a thirteen-year-old girl. She was a middle-school student and was at the county hospital on life support.

The girl, Jessica Jones, and her mother were on their way to school that morning when a late model Cadillac hit their car and sped off, leaving the scene of the accident. The mother, Connie Jones, tried to catch up to the car to obtain the license plate number. Her daughter jotted the number down in one of her school notebooks. Then Connie passed the Cadillac and headed to the nearest police station so she could report the hit-and-run.

The man in the Cadillac then decided to chase them down. When he caught up with them, he fired two shots. One of the bullets went through the back windshield and hit Jessica in the head.

She was life-flighted to the hospital in critical condition and was placed on a respirator. The doctors had declared her brain-dead, but her heart was still beating and her mother didn't want to pull the plug just yet.

Lloyd couldn't imagine what he would do if something like that happened to Bria, who was only four years older than Jessica. He also couldn't imagine the pain that Jessica's mother must be going through. But, since she had the license plate number, the police were at least able to locate the man who fired the shots.

Ed wanted Lloyd to go to the scene of the crime to look for and interview witnesses. That's where Lloyd was headed now. The shooting had occurred in the Heights area of Houston, not far from downtown.

When Lloyd arrived at the crime scene, he could see a small group of people gathered around. A cluster of mementos and notes from well-wishers had already been placed at the site, along with teddy bears and flowers. He parked and then approached the people who had assembled. He introduced himself to a woman who appeared eager to talk. She was in her early thirties, and was wearing jeans and a Houston Rockets t-shirt.

"I'm Lloyd Palmer of the *Houston Ledger*. Did you see what happened?" Lloyd asked, as he took out his digital recorder, pressed the record button and put it near her mouth.

"Yes, sir. I was putting my garbage outside for pickup when two cars went by. I turned around and saw the man in the Cadillac shoot at the car in front of him," she said.

"When the shots went through the windshield, the lady pulled over and then screamed. Her poor child was shot in the head and unconscious. She was crying and calling for help. I called 911 and then tried to comfort her and

help her with her daughter, who had blood gushing from her head."

"The man in the Cadillac didn't even stop. He sped off and left that poor woman. Didn't try to help her or nothin.'"

"Is that what you saw, Ms . . . ?" Lloyd asked another lady who was standing close by.

"The name is Charlotte Sims, sir. It's just like Angela said," she replied, pointing to the woman who had just spoken. Ms. Sims was a bit older, in her fifties, and was wearing a jogging suit and sneakers.

"I couldn't believe that man didn't stop. I tried to get some of the numbers off his license plate, but he was going too fast. Then I found out the child had written down the plate number. Her mother was crying uncontrollably. She had a crumpled piece of paper in her hand and gave it to me. I gave it to the police when they got here," she said.

"Could the man in the Cadillac have been shooting in self defense?" asked Lloyd.

"No sir, no way," said Ms. Sims. "She was just driving straight, and he shot at her twice. He's gonna pay for what he's done, in this life or the next."

Lloyd asked each of the ladies to spell their names for his report and then wrote down some observations about the crime scene. He would have to eventually interview Connie Jones about her daughter's shooting, and he really dreaded it. It was unlikely that Ms. Jones would be in any condition to discuss what happened for the next several days. He certainly was not going to intrude on her at the hospital.

His cell phone rang. It was Ed.

"Lloyd, Jessica Jones was just pronounced dead. Are you at the crime scene?"

Even though Lloyd had been told about victims who had died hundreds of times before, he still cringed when Ed told him the news. "I sure am, Ed. I interviewed a couple of women who actually saw the shooting. Have the police arrested the man who did it yet?"

"They're picking him up at his house now," said Ed. "The man's name is Robert Conrad. He didn't resist arrest or anything and is being taken to jail downtown for processing. He'll probably be charged with felony murder or criminally negligent homicide."

"Lloyd, I want you to go to the hospital. Interview the medical staff who treated Jessica. They're not supposed to tell us much, but you can usually get the nurses or orderlies to give you some information. Slip them twenty bucks and you'll be surprised how much they'll talk.

"Also, talk to her mother. She's probably in bad shape, but you may be able to get a few words out of her."

"Ed, it's completely inappropriate to go the hospital when the mother, if she is still there, will be in anguish. We should respect her time of grief."

"We're in the news business, and the mother's reaction to her daughter's death is news," barked Ed. "Just do it and report back to me," he added, right before he hung up.

Lloyd knew what he had to do. He got in his car and headed toward the hospital. He knew Jessica had been in the Intensive Care Unit, so he called the hospital to see where ICU was located. When he got to the hospital, he wanted to be able to go directly to the correct floor as quickly as possible to speak with hospital personnel before a shift change. The hospital operator said ICU was on the fourth floor.

He arrived at the hospital and took the elevator to the fourth floor. There were two nurses at the nurses' station and Lloyd spoke to the one who appeared to be doubling as a receptionist. "Can you direct me to Jessica Jones' room?" he asked.

"Sir, are you a member of the family?"

"No. I'm Lloyd Palmer and I'm a reporter with the *Ledger*. I just wanted to make sure my information is correct for the story I'm working on," he said. "Is Ms. Jones still here?"

"Mr. Palmer, Ms. Jones' family members took her home a few minutes ago, and you know that we cannot provide any medical details because of doctor/patient privilege," she said.

"Are you able to at least tell me the time of death? That's not classified, and I can find that out from the coroner's office anyway."

The nurse keyed the patient's name into the computer and found the time of death. "Jessica passed away at 11:15 a.m. The poor girl never had a chance," said the nurse.

"Thank you, m'am," said Lloyd. "Where is the men's room, please?"

"It's around the corner, Mr. Palmer."

Lloyd turned the corner, but he had no intention of going to the men's room. He wanted to see if any of the nurses on the floor had more information, but he wanted to be out of earshot of the nurse at the front desk, who seemed to run things by the book. He spotted a nurse walking in his direction and stopped her.

"Miss, I'm here from the *Ledger* and I was wondering if you knew anything about Jessica Jones."

"That was the girl in room 412. She passed away a little while ago. Her mother and other family members were here at the end. They practically had to carry Ms. Jones out of here, she was so distraught," the nurse said.

"Is there anything else you think I should know?" asked Lloyd.

"Well, the man who fired the shots called the floor to speak with Ms. Jones."

"He did?"

"Yes, but Ms. Jones refused to take the call. He said he had no idea that a child was in the car and thought someone was chasing him. He said he was really sorry, but it was too little, too late," she said.

"I appreciate this information and here's twenty dollars for your trouble," said Lloyd, holding the twenty-dollar-bill in his outstretched hand.

"I don't want your money, mister. I just want the public to know what happened," she said. "No mother should have to put her child in the ground. But please don't use my name or I could get in serious trouble."

It was like that sometimes. Some people were willing to provide information because they needed to clear their consciences or thought they were being good citizens. As long as they could be identified as an anonymous source, they were okay with it. But when she said, "Don't use my name," Lloyd was reminded of Hamisi.

Lloyd had most of the information he needed to file his story. He went to the hospital cafeteria, took out his laptop and started pecking out the story. He was relieved that he didn't run into Ms. Jones at the hospital, but he had enough first-hand information about her reaction to make his story credible in Ed's eyes.

A few hours passed, and it was 3:00 p.m. when Lloyd was finally done. He e-mailed the story to Ed and packed everything up to go home. He was leaving just in time to beat the rush hour traffic.

After going a few miles on the freeway, Lloyd approached the 610 Loop, and Hamisi again came to his mind. It would only take him a few miles out of his way to stop by Hamisi's apartment building and talk to him. Lloyd wasn't sure he was at home and didn't have the phone number to call him, but he wanted to take a chance on seeing him again. If Hamisi was going to play a significant role in Lloyd's life, he wanted to get things started — sooner rather than later.

CHAPTER 6

Lloyd arrived at Hamisi's apartment building and took the elevator to the fifteenth floor. He remembered that Hamisi's apartment number was 1508 and he knocked on the door. After a few seconds, Hamisi opened the door slightly. "Hello, Mr. Palmer. Are you still writing the report about my dearly departed neighbor?" he asked.

"Call me Lloyd, please. No, I finished that story on the same day I was here. I actually came to talk with you. The other day you said I could come by if I needed to see you, and I felt like I needed to do that," Lloyd said. He noticed that Hamisi was again wearing the head covering he had worn on Friday.

"Come in, then, and have a seat. I knew you would be back, but I didn't expect you this soon," said Hamisi. "Would you like some tea or anything else to drink, Lloyd?"

"Tea would be great," said Lloyd.

Hamisi left the room to prepare the tea and Lloyd had a chance to look around the apartment. There were two framed maps of what appeared to be Africa on the walls, but the countries were in different locations than those on the traditional world maps. Some of the countries also had different names and boundaries.

On the fireplace mantel, there was a golden goblet with etchings on it, which could have been Arabic or some other ancient language. There was also a large Bible on the coffee table, which appeared to be an antique. Lloyd leafed through the pages and noticed that only the Old Testament was included.

Lloyd wasn't a particularly religious man, but he was familiar with the Bible and its Testaments – Old and New. He went to church on most Sundays and believed in God but was skeptical about some of the things that seemed to go on in most churches. His observation was that there appeared to be more hypocrisy among churchgoers than there was among some people he'd met who were either agnostic or atheist. And some of the pastors seemed more like street hustlers than men who were called by God.

His wife, Stephanie, was a very committed Christian, though, and made sure Bria was in church every week. He didn't want to put a damper on her faith and kept most of his thoughts about church and religion to himself.

Hamisi entered the room carrying a tray. On the tray was a ceramic teapot, two ceramic cups and small containers of sugar, honey and cream. "How do you like your tea?" asked Hamisi.

"I'll take a little honey and nothing else," replied Lloyd.

Hamisi poured hot water into each of the cups and placed an herbal tea bag in each. Once the tea had steeped, he placed the teabags on a saucer and then gave Lloyd his full attention.

"Now tell me, what can I do for you?"

"Would you mind if I asked you a few questions about your country and your religion? Your clothing reminds me of those worn by Jews and I was wondering if you had any connection to the Jewish faith," said Lloyd.

"That depends. Are you asking these questions as a reporter or as a man?" asked Hamisi.

"Well, I will admit that, as a reporter, my curiosity is piqued by your appearance, your wisdom, and some of the items in your home. But I am also interested as a man, as an American, in finding out more about Africa and some of its history," said Lloyd.

"I promised you that I will not publish anything you tell me, including your name, without your permission."

"You strike me as a man of integrity, so I will answer some of your questions," said Hamisi, as he paused thoughtfully. "Yes, I am Jewish. There are many of us in Zimbabwe and we are known as the Lemba Jews."

"You mean you're Jewish like the Jews in America who worship on Saturday and don't eat pork?"

"I cannot speak for the Jews here in America. They are of European descent and our history dates back much further than the recorded history on the continent of Europe. We came from Senna, which is on the other side of the Pusela. As told by our forefathers, we were on a big boat and then a terrible storm nearly destroyed us all. This dates back to our ancestor, Solomon," said Hamisi.

"We do observe the two practices you mentioned; we have a holy day, the seventh day of the week," Hamisi continued. "We are not allowed to eat pork or the food of the Gentiles, and milk is to be drunk separately from meat dishes."

Lloyd raised his palm toward Hamisi, as if motioning him to stop. "Wait a minute. You mean that there is a group of black Jews in Zimbabwe who are descendants of Solomon? Can you prove it?"

"Can the Jews in America today prove who they are?" asked Hamisi. "Our proof is in our history, the words of our ancestors, which have been passed down for more than five thousand years. Why would we lie about such a thing?"

"People make up stories all the time about themselves. They lie about their income, their education, where they were born. You name it, people will lie about it," said Lloyd.

"Perhaps that is true in your country. But I am one of the honored men among our people. I was trained by my father, and he was trained by his father, and his father before him, back for one hundred generations, to maintain the history of the Lemba people," said Hamisi.

"Do you have any books that you can show me that chronicle your history?" asked Lloyd. "If your ancestors and your tribe have been around for more than 5,000 years, there has to be something written in a book about it."

"Once we had a book, but the book was lost. Our oral tradition is equal to or better than any book," said Hamisi.

"The other day when you were here you gave me the impression that you believe something published in a newspaper or book has more validity than our oral tradition. Let me ask you something. Does your newspaper sometimes print information in stories that later turns out to be false?"

"Well, sure. We make mistakes, but we always correct them once they are discovered," said Lloyd.

"Yes, but the first story you printed with the false information is published and distributed to the public. It becomes part of your archives. If someone later reads it, he will believe it is true, as he will not know that the facts were corrected the following week, or whenever you discovered the error," said Hamisi.

"And what about the devastation that can be caused and the reputations that can be destroyed because of the false story? That cannot possibly be corrected."

Hamisi pressed forward with his inquiries. "Do you put the corrections on the front page?"

"Well, no. They are usually on the inside, after the major news of the day is reported," said Lloyd.

"So you do not think it is important to let the same people who read the original story know that you made an error? Or is it just that you are embarrassed by the mistake and want as few people as possible to know about it?"

Lloyd shifted his weight in his seat, becoming somewhat irritated by Hamisi's probing questions. "With all due respect, Mr. Hamisi, what is your point?"

"Since you are questioning the validity of our oral tradition, I am showing you the fallacy of the written word, which can be completely untrue but have more impact since it can be widely distributed and, thus, influences many more people," said Hamisi.

"And what if the error is not discovered? What happens to false information that is published by your newspaper, archived and never discovered to be untrue, but is false nonetheless? It may eventually find its way into some book that is published or be used for historical information and the lie is perpetuated for years to come."

"Okay. Let's say that I believe your oral tradition. What else can you tell me about the Lemba people?" asked Lloyd, as he took his note pad out of his pocket. He thought the use of a recording device might make Hamisi less willing to speak freely.

"As I said, our oral tradition speaks of a land called Senna, which is now believed to be the country of Yemen. We built Senna Two and Senna Three. These were in Africa. We do not know where Pusela is. I think it means the sea."

"We came from Senna, we crossed Pusela," Hamisi repeated. "Solomon sent his ships to get gold from Ophir, that is Zimbabwe. Some of the Jews who went on those boats stayed in Africa. That is the origin of the Lemba people. Our name means 'those who avoid eating with others.' Like the Jews of America, we keep apart from the Gentiles."

"I am familiar with the book called *Roots* by Alex Haley that was published several years ago in your country," Hamisi continued. "Just like Kunta Kente, who was Haley's ancestor, our history is based on oral tradition. But it is quite accurate and verifiable."

"Our oral tradition says that we settled in the great city of Kimbabwe. The wall that was built there hundreds of years ago still stands.

"It was built brick by brick, but with no mortar or cement, something that is unheard of among architects today. Archeologists still do not know how it was done, but it shows the tremendous intellect and mechanical expertise of our ancestors."

"How long have you been in the United States?" asked Lloyd.

"I came here three years ago as part of a State Department effort to forge a better relationship with the government of Zimbabwe. In my country, the Lemba people are very learned. Many of us are professors, doctors and lawyers," said Hamisi.

"What about your wife, your family? Are they here with you?"

"My wife passed away several years ago. She was Lemba also, and I decided not to remarry. You see, we are required to marry someone who is Lemba; otherwise, my potential wife would have to go through a very difficult initiation ceremony. Many women do not survive the ritual or are crippled during the process. I have two sons; both of them are still in Zimbabwe and will become honored men when their time arrives."

"When you say some women are crippled by the process, what do you mean?"

"In many Lemba tribes, women who wish to marry a Lemba man have to crawl through a hole in an ant hill. The idea is that the ants will sting and suck off all the pig blood that this non-Lemba woman has eaten in her life. Then branches are placed over her and a fire is lit on top of her. It is hoped that the fire will burn the contamination and then, just before she is roasted, they push off the branches and throw her into the river to get purified."

Lloyd's expression was one of incredulity. "Are you serious? That sounds gruesome. Why in the world would a woman put herself through all that just to get married?"

"A Lemba man is considered to be among the most wise and prosperous males in many African tribal cultures. The woman knows that if a Lemba is her husband, all of her needs and that of her children and extended family will be met."

"It's still hard to believe that someone would actually volunteer for such a ceremony. It's a wonder that any of them even survive it."

"Most do not," said Hamisi, "but it is a custom that had been part of our heritage for centuries."

Lloyd checked his watch and saw that it was getting close to six o'clock. "You've given me some intriguing information, Mr. Hamisi. If you don't mind, I'd like to digest this and do a little research of my own. I'm not familiar with some of the places you've mentioned."

"Most of my reporting has been on local issues, but I'm trying to branch out and write some engaging stories where the setting is outside the Houston area. May I come by to see you again in a few days? Better still, would you give me your phone number. That way, I can call before stopping by."

"As long as you honor your agreement not to publish my name, then you may return," said Hamisi. "You are a very interesting man, and I get a feeling from you that you can be trusted."

"You have my word that I will keep the information confidential. I am considering writing a story, but I will not release anything you have told me without permission," said Lloyd.

Hamisi wrote down his phone number and gave it to Lloyd. Then the two of them shook hands. "It has been a pleasure meeting you, Mr. Hamisi, and I hope we can become friends."

"For us to become friends, our relationship must endure the test of time," said Hamisi, "so we shall see."

Lloyd left the apartment nearly in a daze. Hamisi was arguably one of the most interesting men he had ever met.

CHAPTER 7

Lloyd got home at about seven o'clock and his adrenaline was supercharged. He wanted to talk to someone about Hamisi and their conversation, and Stephanie was the logical choice. She knew very little about news reporting, other than reading the newspaper each day. She also tended to be very practical—always thinking about security and stability. That was important to him too, but he wanted to break free of some of the monotony he was locked into by his day-to-day activities. He'd decided to broach the subject carefully at dinner.

When he walked through the front door, he could already smell the aromas of whatever Stephanie was preparing for dinner. He walked into the kitchen and gave Stephanie a hug from behind.

"I thought I heard you come in," said Stephanie. "How was everything at work today?"

"You know, same old, same old. What's for dinner?" asked Lloyd, as he kissed Stephanie on the cheek.

"We're having shrimp creole with salad and garlic bread. It's almost ready."

"Where's Bria? Is she upstairs studying?" asked Lloyd.

"She went to one of her classmates' houses to work on a group project they have in history class. She should be home no later than eight o'clock," said Stephanie.

"That works out because I wanted to talk to you about something. I had an interesting conversation with someone today."

"Oh, yeah? Who was it?" she asked.

"It's a man that I met last week while I was on assignment. He's actually not connected to the story I was reporting, other than the fact that he lives in the building where the crime took place. He's some sort of holy man from Zimbabwe, a tribe called the Lemba people who are somehow connected to the Jews."

"Really. It seems I read something about African Jews several years ago when some of them were airlifted to Israel," she said. "I don't remember any details, though. What did he say?" Stephanie began scooping the food from the pots on the stove into the serving dishes. She then placed the serving dishes on the table.

"He's from a family who retains the oral history of his tribe. He says their history goes all the way back to Solomon from the Old Testament. He even has some artifacts in his apartment and wears the traditional Jewish skull cap that I've seen men wear. On top of that, he talks in riddles, but his riddles make sense on a level deeper than I'm used to discussing," said Lloyd.

"Does he have any proof about his lineage? Does he have any certificates showing that he has credentials as a priest, rabbi or whatever they call their holy men?"

"That's just it. I asked him the same thing and he says that his oral tradition *is* proof. He actually proved to me how our newspaper reporting has less validity, in some cases, than the oral history that his people have maintained for centuries. Steph, he says they are taught to recite their history verbatim for one hundred generations. It's really deep."

"Lloyd, maybe you should do some research to see if you can find any corroboration. There has to be some information online somewhere about his tribe or their history. Maybe some historians or archeologists have written reports about it," Steph said, as she and Lloyd sat down at the dinner table and prepared to eat.

"That's what I plan to do," Lloyd said. Then he thought this would be the perfect time to tell Steph that he was planning to write a story and shop it around. She seemed to be genuinely intrigued by the whole thing. Maybe she would be more sympathetic than he was expecting.

"I'm even considering writing a story about it. If the *Ledger* isn't interested, then I could shop it around and see if some magazines or other publications want to publish it." There. He'd said it. Lloyd was testing the waters to see how Steph would react. He knew he could do this on his own, behind her back, but it would be so much easier to have her support.

"Isn't that against company policy?"

Steph had always been very cautious, which had made Lloyd apprehensive about telling her in the first place. She was always worried about him going against the grain at work and possibly losing his job. "No, as long as we give the *Ledger* the right of first refusal, meaning they get to decline publication first, then we can pitch it to whomever we like."

"Well, then, go for it, Lloyd. You're a good writer and you've been talking about expanding your horizons. Who knows? Some other newspaper or news organization might read the story and offer you a position with a higher salary and more benefits," she said.

This was certainly more than Lloyd had hoped for. Steph was actually giving him her blessing to pursue the story about Hamisi.

"You didn't tell me the man's name," said Stephanie. "What is it?"

"Hamisi," said Lloyd. "Rudo Hamisi."

CHAPTER 8

Lloyd got to work the next morning around nine o'clock and began his usual routine of checking e-mails and voice mail messages. Ed hadn't given him an assignment yet, so Lloyd decided to browse the Internet to see if he could find anything about the Lemba tribe that Hamisi described.

Lloyd entered the phrase in the Google search box and, to his surprise, hundreds of listings appeared. It turned out that Hamisi was telling the truth—the Lemba tribe did actually exist, and Lloyd was determined to fill in the blanks about the details.

He scanned the first couple of entries and there was a *New York Times* article from May 1999 about the Lemba, a Bantu-speaking people of southern Africa, who say they were led out of Judea by a man called Buba. The tribe practiced circumcision, kept one day a week holy and avoided eating pork or pig-like animals, such as the hippopotamus.

Even more fascinating was information about a team of geneticists who had studied the DNA of some of the Lemba males. These scientists found that many Lemba men carry in their male chromosomes a set of DNA markers distinctive of descendants of Aaron, the elder brother of the biblical Moses.

In fact, Lemba males, on average, had more DNA markers of the strain associated with Jewish priests than do most of the European Jews. This added even more validity to Hamisi's claims.

Hamisi had said that the Lemba people were very cloistered and did very little mixing with other tribes. If they were able to maintain a consistent gene pool within their group, this could explain the relative purity of their genetic markers.

The article mentioned a professor, Dr. Joseph Gastalt, who had actually traveled to Africa, met some of the Lemba clan and lived among them for a few months. Gastalt had documented his findings in a book and had confirmed some of the narrative Hamisi had told Lloyd. Gastalt was a tenured professor of genetics at the University of Chicago, and Lloyd jotted down his name. He'd do some research later to get the professor's e-mail address and phone number so he could contact him and find out more.

Lloyd saw his friend, Charles, approaching and quickly switched his screen to another browser window. He wasn't yet ready to let anyone else at work know about his project.

"Hey, Lloyd. What's up?"

"Nothing much. I'm just checking my e-mail to see if there are any story leads. What about you?"

"Oh, I've been covering this story about a child pornography ring that seems to have started in the Houston area, but has since spread worldwide through a password-protected web site," said Charles.

"I hate dealing with the sleaze balls who do this sort of stuff, but the paper's circulation always seems to go up whenever we do one of these stories. Ed's had me working on this one for the past week."

"Better you than me, man," said Lloyd. "I'm not sure I could interview any of these guys without punching them in the face first."

"They'll only speak to me off the record with no photographs or recordings. They know that their actions are abominable, but they all say they can't seem to stop. It's an addiction, an obsession. Some of them have an arrest record for child pornography or sex crimes, but most of them have been operating under the police radar for years."

"By the way, I'm going to happy hour over at the Oasis after work," said Charles. "Wanna come?" The Oasis Bar & Grill was a popular hangout for *Ledger* employees. Over the years, Lloyd and Charles had gone there together frequently after work.

"I might just do that. I haven't been to happy hour in a while and it might do me some good to have a few drinks and relax," said Lloyd. "I'll meet you there at six o'clock."

Charles looked up and saw Audrey headed their way. "Don't turn around now, man, but Audrey looks like she's about to pounce on you from behind."

"Good grief," Lloyd responded as he sighed deeply and turned around. He didn't want Audrey sneaking up on him and catching him off guard. She took the last few steps toward his desk.

"Good morning, Audrey. What can I do for you?"

"Hi, Lloyd," she said, as she bent down toward him, her substantial cleavage only a few inches away from his face. Lloyd had to will himself to look into her eyes and not at her boobs.

"Ed wants you to come to his office. He says he has a big assignment for you," she said, and then she moistened her lips.

"Okay, thanks," Lloyd replied as he gingerly inched his way around her and walked toward Ed's office. Halfway there, he turned around and said, "I'll see you at six o'clock, Charles," and then continued towards Ed's office.

"If I'm not there, just wait for me," replied Charles.

Lloyd walked into Ed's office. "Audrey told me you wanted to see me, Ed. Whatcha got for me?"

"The authorities just found the bodies of a couple in Pasadena, shot execution style. They were babysitting their nieces when they were shot," said Ed.

"The girls weren't killed too, were they?" asked Lloyd, as he braced for the worst.

"Fortunately, no. They were unharmed. But the girls were the first to see the bodies when their mother came to pick them up. She rang the doorbell, and the girls came downstairs. Their mother had been calling for over an hour, and when there was no answer, she came by to pick up her girls to see what was going on."

"How old are the girls?" asked Lloyd.

"They are six and eight years old. Really tragic. I'll need you to high tail it to Pasadena right now."

"I'm on my way," said Lloyd. "Anything else I should be aware of?"

"The couple doesn't appear to have a criminal background, but you can double check that with the county and state authorities," said Ed.

As Lloyd left Ed's office, boarded the elevator and pressed the lobby button, he wondered if the victims were African American. Ed normally sent him on assignments that occurred in black neighborhoods or where the victims and/or perpetrators were black. If the victims weren't black, that usually meant that no other reporters were available or that they had all been assigned to other stories. Ed was a real imbecile, but at least he was predictable.

Pasadena was about twenty miles east of Houston, but traffic was heavy so it took Lloyd about an hour to get there. He found the address with relative ease; and once he was nearby, the police vehicles and yellow crime scene tape let him know he was in the right place. After he parked, he used his laptop to get some information on the victims before going inside.

The victims were John and Sharonda Price. According to the information he found online, they had lived in their subdivision for five years.

Some of the neighbors were still milling around outside. Lloyd exited the car and approached one of the men he saw who appeared to be in his thirties. He was wearing one of those throw-back sports jerseys and had on a baseball cap, which he wore backwards.

"Excuse me, sir. I'm with the *Houston Ledger* and I wanted to ask you a few questions. Did you know Mr. and Mrs. Price?"

"I've been living across the street from them since they moved in five years ago. I can't believe this happened in our neighborhood. It's usually so quiet," he said.

"Did you notice anything that looked like criminal activity near their home? Ever see any suspicious looking characters, Mister . . . ?"

"The name is Harold, sir, Harold Grimley. No, man, they were straight up legit. Church-going folks. John used to do car repairs and maintenance as a sideline business, but his main job was working at the post office.

"And Sharonda, man, she was good people. Always had a kind word and helping people out when they needed it. Maybe it was a robbery," he said, making the statement as if it could have been either an assertion or a question.

"The police are investigating that, but it appears that they were shot by intruders. Someone forced his way into the home, so it could have been a robbery, as you say," said Lloyd.

"This is going to make people very scared," said Harold. "We'll have to start doing a neighborhood watch and installing burglar bars on the doors and windows. Maybe even traffic cameras at the entrances to the subdivision. I still can't believe this happened right across the street. It could have been me and mine, man."

"I'm sorry about what happened to your neighbors. If you think of anything, here's my card," Lloyd said, as he handed Grimley one of his *Ledger* business cards.

Lloyd went to the front door of the Prices' home, which was wide open, and walked in. The police and forensics team were still there taking blood samples and collecting other evidence.

The place had been ransacked and blood was splattered all over the walls and floor. Some of the smaller pieces of furniture were turned over and the drawers in the china cabinet were open. The bodies had already been removed, but it was clear that murders had been committed there.

From the looks of the place, a lot of noise was made when the intruders entered the house. Lloyd thought it was amazing that the two girls had not awakened during the ruckus and come downstairs. The fact that they were sound sleepers probably saved their lives.

"Sheriff, I'm Lloyd Palmer with the *Ledger*. What can you tell me so far?"

"It looks like a gangland style killing, but the neighbors all say the couple was squeaky clean," said the sheriff. "One of them told me the Prices wouldn't even accept stolen property. If somebody came by selling something that didn't seem legit, they would turn them away."

"Looks like it could have just been a simple robbery, and the hoodlums shot the Prices so there wouldn't be any witnesses. It's a shame, too. From all indications, they seemed to be a very nice couple—church-going and everything."

"What time did the murders occur?" asked Lloyd. "Did anybody see anything?"

"Since they were killed in the middle of the night, at around 1:00 a.m., the neighbors were asleep. The perpetrators entered through the back door. Looks like they picked the lock and came in. We haven't found anyone in the neighborhood who heard or saw anything."

Lloyd had already spoken with one neighbor but needed some corroboration from others. The sheriff's information was similar to what Mr. Grimley, who lived across the street, had told him. But it was always better to obtain at least two first-hand sources for his news stories, so Lloyd went back outside and decided to canvas the neighborhood some more.

There were still some residents milling around the cul-de-sac, including Grimley, who was engaged in a conversation with a young man in his twenties. Lloyd walked toward them, stood next to Grimley, and said, "Mr. Grimley, is this one of your neighbors?"

"Yes," replied the young man, who appeared to be a little nervous. "Who are you?"

"This man is a reporter with the *Ledger*, Carl," said Grimley. "He's writing a story about the Price murders."

"Oh," the young man said, as he appeared to relax a bit. "I live a couple of houses over. You see the house over there with the red brick exterior?" he said, as he pointed to a house that was on the opposite side of the street and two houses toward the east.

"It's a shame what happened to those people. I heard that someone picked the lock on the back door, and that's how they got in."

Lloyd hesitated a moment because he had been told that by the sheriff on the scene, but as far as he knew the information hadn't yet been made public. "You say that someone picked the lock on the back door?" asked Lloyd. "How did you know about that?"

Carl fidgeted as he realized that he may have said too much. "I just heard somebody say that, man. How else would the robbers have gotten into the house?"

"Well, they could have gotten in through a window or someone could have actually let them in," said Lloyd. He let Carl digest that for a few seconds before continuing.

"Can you spell your first and last names for the news report?"

"I'd rather you not publish my name, man. I don't want to get involved. The robbers might come back looking for the people who talked," Carl responded.

Lloyd scribbled in his notepad concerning Carl's demeanor and the location of his home. As a reporter, he sometimes uncovered information about a crime that he could then pass on to the authorities. The general public was unaware of how often folks in the news business actually helped law enforcement officials solve crimes.

Carl definitely had some connection to the murders. It may have been a casual connection, but Carl was associated with the killers in some way. As the old adage goes, the perpetrator always returns to the scene of the crime.

Lloyd made his way toward the Prices' home and looked back at the small crowd that still remained. Carl was walking briskly back to his house. Once inside, Lloyd spoke to the sheriff in charge.

"Sheriff, I didn't get your name before but I wanted to ask you something."

"The name is Logan, Mr. Palmer, Jack Logan. What can I do for you?"

"Have any details about the crime been released to the press or published anywhere yet?"

"The only details we've released have been the names of the victims and the method in which they were killed. Other than that, we are gathering the forensics data and will be holding a press conference late this afternoon."

"I asked because you had mentioned that it looked as though the lock on the back door had been picked by the people who broke in. Have you provided that detail to anyone else?"

"Actually, no, because we had just made that determination when you arrived."

"Then I may have a lead for you. I interviewed a young man outside who knew that the locks on the back door were picked. How would he have known that if he didn't have something to do with the killings?"

"Did you get his name or his address?"

"Well, he wouldn't give me his last name, but he said his first name is Carl and he lives two doors down the street in the house with the red brick front."

"We'll get right on it," said the sheriff, as he spoke into the radio that was affixed to his shirt on his left shoulder.

Lloyd went to his car to type out the story on his laptop and file it with the editor. Going to the scene of yet another gruesome crime had been a downer; he'd felt a bout of depression coming on as soon as he crossed the Prices' threshold. But helping to solve the crime lifted his spirits a bit. Once he met Charles at the Oasis and had a few drinks, his spirits would be elevated even more.

CHAPTER 9

Lloyd headed to the Oasis Bar and Grill and parked next to Charles' car, which he spotted as soon as he entered the parking lot. Although it was a Tuesday evening, the parking lot was almost full. He entered the Oasis and saw Charles sitting at the bar, with a beautiful, long-legged woman on each side of him. One was a blonde and the other a brunette. Charles was a magnet for the pretty ones, but, so far, he was a confirmed bachelor.

"Hi, Charles," Lloyd said as he approached the bar. He stood beside Charles and smiled at both of the ladies. "What are you drinking?"

"Tequila on the rocks," said Charles. "Why not join me?"

"Man, the last time I drank some tequila I woke up with a migraine headache the next day, so I'm going to pass," said Lloyd. "Bartender, can you get me a rum and coke please?"

"Charles, I'd like to talk to you about something. Do you think we can have a little privacy?" Lloyd whispered in Charles' ear.

"Sure, Lloyd," said Charles and then turned toward the ladies. "Ladies, would you mind waiting for me in that booth over there?" he said, as he pointed across the room. "Lloyd and I need to talk shop for a few minutes, and then I'll be right over."

"Don't take too long, Charles," said the brunette, as she put the cherry from her drink into her mouth, bit it slowly, and then put the stem back in the glass. "We'll be waiting," she said, as she blew him a kiss.

She then winked as she and her buddy sauntered toward the booth. It was obvious she was sending Charles a clear signal about what he could expect later that evening.

Charles watched as they both slowly walked away and then turned his attention to Lloyd. "Those two are super hot. They are no-holds-barred in the bedroom, just like I like 'em. But I know you're married and all, so I won't tempt you with the tantalizing details. Today at the office you seemed as though you wanted to talk about something. What can I do for you, my man?"

"I'm considering writing a story on my own to submit to Ed. If he doesn't like it, I may even pitch it to some other publications.

"My first thought is that he probably won't think my story idea is appropriate for the *Ledger*. I know you've done some writing for other publications in the past, and I just wanted to know how Ed reacted to that."

"Most of the stories I've written were not local. They were human interest stories that had more of a national appeal or were based in cities outside Texas. Ed had no problem with it at all. One time he actually gave me the hookup to the editor of a national magazine who he thought might be interested in the story."

"See, Lloyd, when a reporter from the *Ledger* writes a story that receives national recognition, it's actually good for the paper, even when it's published somewhere else. It raises the *Ledger*'s stature and puts us on par with some of the national newspapers that are quoted all the time, like *The New York Times* and *The Wall Street Journal*.

"If you have a story idea, go for it," said Charles.

"I don't have the same relationship with Ed that you do," replied Lloyd. "He never reprimands you, even when you make mistakes. He just pats you on the back and says, 'You'll work it out next time.' But when I make a mistake, he bites my head off."

"Remember that time you reported that one of the city council members was involved in a murder-for-hire scheme. It turned out that she wasn't involved at all and that your source had some sort of vendetta against her, so he supplied you with false information.

She threatened to sue the paper for defamation of character and libel. The *Ledger* had to print a front-page retraction and a full-page apology. Ed gave you a tongue-lashing, but no reprimand or demotion or anything."

"Ed barks at you because you are too timid with him, Lloyd. If you stand up to him once in a while, he'll back off," said Charles. "You are way too cautious. If you don't take chances every now and then and push the envelope, you'll never know what's possible."

Lloyd really liked Charles, and Charles had always watched Lloyd's back at work. But Charles just didn't understand that there were two different sets of rules — one for the white boys at work, and one for everyone else. The two of them were operating in parallel universes.

Charles could use his charm to break the rules without receiving even a slap on the wrist. Lloyd had to toe the company line and could make few mistakes. He felt as though he was always one or two mistakes away from the unemployment line.

"I do plan to work on the story, but I still haven't made up my mind about approaching Ed. I might have more success shopping it elsewhere," Lloyd said.

"What's the story about? Anything I can help with or that we can work on together?" asked Charles.

"I'd rather keep it to myself for now, at least until I work out more of the details. Besides the local guy that I'm working with is very protective of his identity."

"Well, whatever you decide to do, I've got you covered. You can come to me for help or to bounce off ideas anytime. Let's toast to your success with your new writing venture. May you win the Pulitzer Prize," said Charles, as he raised his glass to toast Lloyd's.

"To a Pulitzer," said Lloyd, as their glasses clanked and they each gulped down the contents.

"If you don't mind, Lloyd, I don't want to keep the honeys waiting," said Charles. "I'll see you tomorrow at work." He got down off the barstool and looked in the direction of the booth where the blonde and the brunette were sitting.

"Go ahead, man. No problem. If I were in your shoes, I'd be rushing over there myself."

Lloyd ordered another drink from the bartender and nursed it for the next half hour. He wasn't sure in which direction this story about Hamisi and the Lemba people would take him. But he was going to start working on it tomorrow.

CHAPTER 10

Lloyd decided to go into work early the next day and arrived at the office about eight o'clock. During the drive downtown, he'd given some thought to how he would proceed with his research for the story about the Lemba tribe. He'd do most of his work at home or on his laptop when he was out on assignment. On the office computer, he never knew who might be monitoring his online activity, and he didn't want to raise any red flags with Ed before he was ready.

But he wanted to find out more about the professor who had spent two years living with the Lemba people. After arriving at work, Lloyd did an online search for Dr. Joseph Gastalt and found his curriculum vitae and his web site. On Gastalt's schedule of events, he had posted Houston as a destination within a couple of weeks. It appeared that Professor Gastalt was going to speak at a Rice University symposium on African tribes. Lloyd noted Gastalt's phone number and planned to call him later that week to schedule a face-to-face interview during the professor's visit.

Lloyd's phone rang and he answered it. "This is Lloyd Palmer."

"Hello, Mr. Palmer. This is Sheriff Jack Nolan of the Pasadena Police Department. We met the other day at the Price home."

"Oh, yes. I remember you. What can I do for you Sheriff Nolan?"

"I just called to thank you for your tip the other day. Your information got us several steps closer to solving the crime. The gentleman you referred to us was Carl Jenkins. After we questioned him, he confessed that he knew the men who broke into the house.

"He appears to have had only indirect involvement with the crime, but he gave us the primary suspects' names and addresses. We've picked them up and brought them in for questioning. It is likely that their fingerprints will match those found at the scene or they left behind some DNA. It might have taken us weeks to solve these murders if you hadn't helped us."

"I'm glad I could be of assistance," said Lloyd. "The Price family deserves justice—speedy justice at that. Thank you for calling, Sheriff Nolan."

Lloyd hung up the phone and called Ed on his extension. Ed picked up on the first ring. "Ed, I've got some news about the Price homicide. The Sheriff just called and said they'd picked up the perpetrators. Do you want me to start working on a follow-up story?"

"Yes, you can file that one this afternoon once you get the details. But I have another story for you to work on as well. This one is breaking news in progress. Would you come into my office right away?"

Lloyd hung up and walked quickly toward Ed's office. "What's it about, Ed?"

"The police have just started a man hunt in River Oaks and the streets adjacent to it. It seems that one of the residents of the community was wheeling her baby in a stroller when a black male driving a black SUV stopped, jumped out of the car and snatched her baby out of the stroller. She couldn't give many details about the kidnapper, other than he was dark-skinned, of medium height and with a medium build. But she's very hysterical, and the baby was only two months old."

The River Oaks section of Houston was located in the city's geographic center and was one of the wealthiest communities in the state of Texas. Its residents had a lot of political and social clout, and few blacks had ever lived there. Even some wealthy athletes and celebrities were turned away when they made inquiries to buy a home. The cost of entry was not only financial, but one needed a certain pedigree to even obtain an appointment with a real estate agent to view homes available for sale.

"Have the police confirmed that this actually took place, Ed?" asked Lloyd. "It sounds a lot like the case in South Carolina several years back where a woman said a black man snatched her two young boys. That woman couldn't give any details either, and it turned out to be a hoax. She was covering up the murder of her own children and using a generic black man as a scapegoat."

"Well, the woman in South Carolina was considered to be trailer park trash, at best. This woman lives in River Oaks. Her husband is friends with the mayor, and the police department and this newspaper are taking it very seriously."

"All I'm saying, Ed, is that I believe the facts should be examined carefully before the Houston police go on some sort of witch hunt. Her description fits nearly half the adult black men in Houston. And, realistically, how far do you think a black man with a two-month-old white baby would get without attracting attention? It just doesn't fit the normal M.O. of a kidnapper. They are usually white males in their twenties or thirties. It is rare that a black male is involved in a kidnapping for ransom."

"That's enough, Lloyd. The woman's name is Christina Pauley and I want you to go to her home in the 14000 block of Del Monte Drive. She lives in the largest house on the block, the one with a veranda on the east side of the house and white columns in front. It's a lovely home. I had cocktails there recently with the Country Club Republicans."

Ed liked to brag about how well connected he was to the rich and famous, even though he wasn't one of them. It made him feel superior.

"I want you to talk to her and get more details on this black boy who took her baby," continued Ed. "I want your story filed by three o'clock today, and I don't want any more lip from you. Is that clear?"

Lloyd wondered if Ed was using the term "boy" because he had information about the approximate age of the alleged kidnapper, or if it was a Freudian slip of the tongue. Lloyd was about to explode inside but had learned over the years not to show his emotions at work. "Yes, Ed. I'll call you when I get there."

CHAPTER 11

The River Oaks section was not far from the *Ledger*'s downtown headquarters, and Lloyd arrived at the Pauley home within about fifteen minutes. There were multiple police vehicles in front of the large circular driveway. The three-story house had a red brick exterior with ivy growing on both sides of the front door.

The white columns that Ed had mentioned were prominent at the front of the house. The lawn was beautifully landscaped with tulips and begonias planted out front. Lloyd rang the doorbell, and a middle-aged Hispanic maid answered.

"Yes, may I help you?"

"I'm Lloyd Palmer with the *Houston Ledger*. I'm here to ask Mrs. Pauley a few questions about the kidnapping."

He showed the maid his identification badge. "Come in, Mr. Palmer," she said with a thick accent. "Mrs. Pauley is anxious to speak with the reporters."

Lloyd thought that was odd. If his daughter, Bria, had been kidnapped, the last thing he'd be interested in would be talking to reporters. The police, yes, but reporters, no. He'd be so consumed with anxiety that finding her would be the only thing on his mind. That made him even more suspicious about the veracity of Mrs. Pauley's claims.

The maid led him into a room that appeared to be the library. An attractive woman in her mid-thirties was sitting on the couch with tissues in her hands. She appeared to have been crying.

"Mrs. Pauley," said the maid, "this is Mr. Palmer from the *Ledger* and he would like to ask you a few questions."

Mrs. Pauley extended her hand to Lloyd. "It's good to meet you, Mr. Palmer. Please have a seat," she said, as she pointed to the area beside her on the sofa. Lloyd sat down.

"I'm sorry to intrude on you during your time of crisis, but our readers will want to know what happened," said Lloyd. "Can you describe how your son was kidnapped?"

"Well, I was taking little Hunter for his morning walk like I usually do. I go a couple of blocks east and then make a complete circle back to the house about four days a week. I get some exercise, and Hunter gets some sun before the mid-day heat sets in," said Mrs. Pauley, as she took a handful of tissues and blew her nose.

"I was in the middle of my walk when a black SUV stopped at the curb beside us. A dark-skinned black man got out, pointed a gun at me and said, 'Give me the baby.'

"I pleaded with him not to take Hunter, but he was pointing the gun at me the whole time. He loosened the stroller strap, removed Hunter from the stroller, put him in the back seat and pulled away."

As Lloyd listened intently, he noticed that there were more holes in Mrs. Pauley's story than there were in a package of Swiss cheese. He could not believe the police had taken her claims seriously, but he let her continue.

"After the car sped off, I screamed for help. I had my cell phone with me and called 911. The police arrived shortly after that."

"Mrs. Pauley, can you give a more detailed description of the man who took Hunter? So far, all you've said is that he was dark-skinned. Can you give his approximate height, weight or age? Did he have any distinctive marks, like tattoos or scars? What was he wearing?"

"It all happened so fast. Let's see, he was medium height, maybe five feet ten inches tall. He was very muscular and was between twenty and thirty years old, I think."

"I wasn't really looking at him that closely because I was very frightened," she continued. "After all, he was pointing a gun at me."

To Lloyd, she seemed to be making things up as she went along. "Can you describe the make or model of the SUV he was driving? Was it a Ford Expedition, a Ford Explorer, or an Escalade? Was it a foreign make, like a Mercedes or a BMW?"

"I really don't know much about cars, but I believe it was a Ford. It was big and black and had tinted windows."

"Was anyone else with him or was he acting alone?"

"When he opened the back door, I didn't see anyone else inside, so I guess he was acting alone."

Lloyd continued with the barrage of questions. "Can you think of a reason why someone would kidnap your child, Mrs. Pauley? Did the kidnapper ask you your name or did he ask for the child's name?"

"We didn't carry on a conversation, if that's what you mean," she replied.

"Mrs. Pauley, what I mean is has he called to make a ransom demand?"

"We haven't received any calls yet, but I'm assuming that he kidnapped Hunter for ransom. We River Oaks residents are constantly targeted by criminals of one sort or another," she said with an air of superiority. "My husband and I just want Hunter back," she said, as she again sobbed into the tissues.

"The only thing is, Mrs. Pauley, how did the kidnapper know who you were? Since Hunter is only two months old, his picture probably has not yet been circulated and, at that age, babies look very much alike."

"I have no idea. He could have been following me and keeping track of when I come and go. As I said, I take Hunter for our neighborhood stroll about four days a week."

"Did the kidnapper have a car seat in the back?"

"I'm not sure. Why do you ask?"

Lloyd could tell that Mrs. Pauley was beginning to get nervous about all of the questions he was asking, another clear sign that she was indeed hiding something. The normal reaction from a mother whose child was missing would have been periodic outbursts of tears coupled with complete cooperation.

"Well, a two-month old baby cannot sit up in the back seat of a car. How did the kidnapper transport Hunter if he didn't have a car seat?"

"I didn't look in the back seat, but he could have laid Hunter down in the back."

"Was Hunter asleep at the time of the kidnapping?"

"No, he was awake, Mr. Palmer. He was playing in the stroller."

"And he didn't cry, scream or show any signs of distress when the stranger picked him up from the stroller and put him the car?"

"Well, Hunter is a very quiet baby, and he doesn't cry that much." She paused and looked at Lloyd intently. "You certainly ask a lot of questions, Mr. Palmer. The police officers didn't ask all of these questions. They just wanted a description of the man who grabbed Hunter, and they've asked me to work with a professional sketch artist so they could circulate a picture of him to all of the law enforcement departments in the area."

"Well, Mrs. Pauley, I'm a reporter, and that's how we develop the details of our stories. We ask a lot of questions. By the way, Mrs. Pauley, where is your husband?"

"He's overseas on a business trip in London closing a major real estate deal. I called him as soon as this happened, and he's on his way back to the States now. His plane should arrive this evening," she said as she blew her nose, once again, into the wad of crumpled tissues in her hand.

"He flies in a private jet, you know; one of the perks of being a top executive at the company."

"Mrs. Pauley, do you have a recent picture of Hunter that I could have so we can include it with the story?"

She perked up a bit then. "Yes. We had some professional photos of Hunter taken a couple of weeks ago, and I'll get one for you."

She stood up and casually strolled out of the room as Lloyd looked around the library. As were most homes of the wealthy, the room was filled with expensive carvings and art. The built-in walnut bookcases included what appeared to be the classics and many first-edition books. Original artwork hung on all four walls. There were a number of Persian throw rugs and a Louis XIV desk.

The police were probably intimidated as soon as they walked in the door. It had been Lloyd's experience that law enforcement officers were trained not to ask the wealthy too many questions when they arrived at a crime scene.

With the political connections the rich possessed, aggressive questioning by a police officer could result in a reprimand, demotion or even a dismissal. No officer wanted to risk losing his pension to cast doubt on a well-connected Houstonian who, even if guilty, could afford high-priced legal representation and beat the rap.

Mrs. Pauley returned with the photo. "Here's a picture of our precious Hunter, Mr. Palmer. We would be eternally grateful for anything the *Ledger* could do to help us apprehend this monster."

"We will certainly let the public know about this, and perhaps someone will see Hunter with the kidnapper and call the authorities. After all, a black man with a white infant in tow should be easy to spot." Lloyd wondered if Mrs. Pauley would notice the implication he was making, but it went right over her head.

"I'll get Maria to show you out," said Mrs. Pauley, referring to the maid who had greeted Lloyd at the door. Lloyd followed her out of the room and was met by Maria at the library's entrance.

"Please come this way, Mr. Palmer," said Maria, as Lloyd followed her to the front door. He turned around and looked at the winding staircase, which dominated the home's entrance.

It was obvious to him that Mrs. Pauley was hiding something, and he wondered how the police were going to respond. It would not be long before he would get his answer.

CHAPTER 12

Ron Singleton was leaving work unusually late for a Wednesday evening. As the chief engineer for Houston's new road construction project, he was finishing up a meeting with some contractors that did not end until seven o'clock. He rarely left the office later than five thirty, and, as he walked to his car, he phoned his wife, Shirley, to let her know he was just leaving.

"Sorry I didn't call you earlier, honey, but the meeting just broke a few minutes ago. These contractors have botched some of the sewer work that needed to be done and it looks like this project is going to be thirty days overdue. I'm going to recommend that we don't use this company again. They've messed up one time too many."

"I was starting to get a little worried, Ron, with all of the law enforcement that's on the road now."

Ron had been in meetings all day and had not heard the news about the Pauley kidnapping. "What do you mean?"

"Haven't you heard, Ron? A River Oaks baby has been kidnapped. The news people are reporting that the kidnapper was a dark-skinned black man in a black SUV. The police have been stopping anybody who remotely fits the description and conducting a vehicle search.

"More than two dozen black men have been arrested already. The NAACP and the New Black Panther Party are both up in arms, but until the baby is found, black men in the city are vulnerable. Since you're in your black Chevy Tahoe and you didn't get home at the usual time, I've been very nervous."

"I'm sure it's not as bad as you say, Shirley. And I have a City of Houston parking sticker on my car so, even if I get stopped, the cops will know that I work for the city."

"Ron, this family lives in River Oaks, which means they have a lot of clout. They're not your average family with an average baby. Please get home as soon as possible."

"I'm headed home now, and I don't have any stops I need to make. I'll be there soon."

Ron hit the end button on his cell phone and slowly pulled out of the downtown parking lot. He had a thirty-minute drive home and had not eaten since lunch time, so he was looking forward to eating whatever Shirley had prepared. He only had to drive about twelve blocks before he reached the on-ramp to the I-45 freeway. Once he got on the freeway, he didn't anticipate any delays.

Ron turned on the Sade CD he had been listening to that morning and had only gone a few blocks when he looked in his rearview mirror and noticed a flashing police light. He certainly had not been speeding, and he assumed that the police wanted him to pull over so they could pass by. When he pulled over, the police car pulled behind him.

Early on, Ron had learned the routine. As a black man in America, he'd learned that he had to be completely passive and non-confrontational as far as law enforcement was concerned. He had known too many people who, because they had done nothing wrong and thought they were in the clear, had challenged the police officer who had stopped them. Things often spiraled out of control and led to an arrest and a court appearance.

In more extreme cases, some Houston drivers had been shot, though none fatally in several years. Unfortunately, the criminal justice system was upside down as far as black men were concerned. They were first presumed to be guilty and they had to prove their innocence.

Ron checked his rearview mirror again, and two police officers emerged from their car. They approached his car from both sides, and he rolled down his window. The officer on the driver's side shined his flashlight into the front seat of Ron's car.

"How can I help you officers?"

"Do you know that your rear tail light is not working?"

"It isn't? I didn't know, officer. I had my car inspected about six months ago and didn't know the bulb had gone out. I'll get it fixed as soon as possible. But I'm curious: Do you routinely stop people who have non-working tail lights?"

"We do when a vehicle fits the description of a car used in the commission of a crime; but, according to the law, we can stop anyone for probable cause. There was a kidnapping this morning and your SUV fits the description of the vehicle used to snatch the little boy."

"My wife mentioned that to me a few moments ago officer when I spoke to her on the phone, but I assure you that I am a law abiding citizen. I'm just getting off of work and I work for the City of Houston. Let me show you my identification," Ron said, as he reached in his suit jacket pocket for his wallet.

Both of the officers pulled their guns out of their holsters and pointed them in his direction. "Hold it right there, buddy. Put your hands up."

"But, officer, I was just reaching for my wallet to show you my identification," said Ron, as he realized that he had made the potentially fatal mistake of making a sudden movement without first requesting permission.

"Put your hands up," the officer said again, this time with more emphasis and volume.

Ron nervously raised both his hands, and the officer on the driver's side opened his door. "Now get out of the car, sir, and face your vehicle."

Humiliated, Ron complied with their instructions and put his hands on the roof of his SUV as the officer searched him from head to toe. The officer reached inside Ron's jacket pocket and removed his wallet.

The officer who had searched Ron handed the wallet to his partner. "Check out his identification, Bob, and make sure there are no warrants for his arrest."

"It says here that his name is Ronald Singleton," said the officer who was on the passenger side of Ron's SUV, as he went to the police car and typed Ron's name and driver's license number into the computer. After a few minutes, the officer in the car returned.

"We are going to have to take you in for questioning and for resisting arrest, Mr. Singleton," said the officer as he placed handcuffs on Ron's wrists.

"Resisting arrest? When did I resist arrest, officer? I was just trying to show you my identification."

"Mr. Singleton, you fit the general description of the kidnapper we've been looking for, and you're driving the type of vehicle that was described. All day, we've been looking for a dark-skinned black male who is about your height and driving a black SUV. Once we get you to the station, if you can account for your whereabouts at 11:00 a.m. today, the charges may be dropped. At that time, you'll be issued a ticket for the busted tail light," said the officer as he opened the back door of the car and motioned for Ron to get inside.

"Officers, if you run my driver's license through the system, you'll see that I don't have any outstanding warrants. I haven't even had a traffic ticket in more than five years," Ron said he lowered his head to get in the back seat. Passing cars slowed down to observe the policemen in action.

"Officers, you're making a mistake," Ron pleaded, to no avail. The police car pulled away from the curb and headed toward the city jail.

Ron had been there once when he had to bail his nephew out of jail for outstanding traffic warrants. He never dreamed he'd be going there himself as a suspected criminal.

CHAPTER 13

As Lloyd sat at home watching the local evening news, Hamisi's words haunted him. Lloyd knew in the depths of his soul that the Pauley kidnapping was a hoax— Mrs. Pauley's account of the facts simply did not add up. Yet, the manhunt for the suspected kidnapper dominated all of the local news stations. CNN had even mentioned it on their Headline News program, but had only included some video footage of the Pauleys from a previous story they had run featuring some of Houston's influential couples.

Hamisi had told him that the information fed to the American masses through the mainstream media often had less validity than the Lemba tribe's oral tradition, and Lloyd had almost laughed at him. Now Lloyd felt as though the joke was on him as he digested the video montage of black men in handcuffs placed into police vehicles and carted off to jail.

The *Ledger* was fully engaged in the news coverage, updating the web site every two hours with new photos and community reaction. The police artist's rendition of the kidnapper was published in the paper and all citizens were encouraged to report anyone looking like the suspect to the authorities. The problem was that the sketch looked more like a cartoon character than a real person—it could be everybody or nobody.

Lloyd had filed the last installment of his story before coming home and would start again early in the morning. But he hadn't seen any news reports questioning the veracity of Mrs. Pauley's tall tale. She was rich and powerful, and her pronouncements were taken at face value.

Residents in Houston's predominantly black neighborhoods felt as though they were under siege. Nearly every black SUV with a black male driver was being stopped and searched, and the arrest rate was well above the norm. So far, no credible leads had been uncovered.

Earlier that day, the mayor held a press conference and pleaded with the citizens to remain calm. And the search was not confined to the Houston city limits, but extended to neighboring suburbs, like Conroe, Humble, The Woodlands, Tomball, Alief, Katy and even Sugar Land. Although dozens of men had been detained, no one had yet been charged with the crime. It seemed that the baby and the perpetrator had simply vanished into thin air.

Lloyd's cell phone rang and he looked at the caller ID. It was Shirley Singleton.

"Hey, Shirley. How are y'all doing over there?"

"Lloyd, I need your help. Ron has been arrested."

Lloyd was stunned. "Shirley, you can't be serious. Arrested for what? Don't tell me he's been caught up in this kidnapping mess?"

Shirley was in tears. "Lloyd, I can't believe this is happening. Ron is one of the most honorable men I know, but the police claim he was resisting arrest. He wanted me to know that he is okay, and he asked me to call you. Lloyd, he wants you to post his bond and pick him up downtown. He didn't want me to come down to the city jail and deal with the hassle of getting him out. Can you take care of this for me?"

"Of course I will, Shirley. Don't you worry. I'll go pick him up, and Ron will be home in no time."

Lloyd hung up the phone and went into the kitchen. He felt even more powerless with his best friend behind bars. Stephanie was in there cleaning up the after dinner mess.

"Steph, Shirley just called. Ron's been arrested, and I'm on my way downtown to post his bond."

Stephanie was removing a plate from the table, but stopped and stood rock still. "Oh, no. I cannot believe this is happening. This whole thing is surreal. It's like something out of a movie, except it is really happening right here in Houston, one of the largest cities in the nation. How's Shirley holding up?"

"She's upset about this, which is to be expected. Ron asked me to go pick him up. He prefers that Shirley wait at home for him."

"I think Bria and I should go over to the house and wait with her, don't you?"

"That would be a good idea. Once Ron is home, we'll come back here together."

Stephanie went upstairs to get Bria, and they all prepared to leave the house. They got to the front door, and Stephanie grabbed her keys from the key rack on the wall. "Everything will be okay, you'll see," said Lloyd, as he embraced them both.

Stephanie and Bria got into Stephanie's car and headed toward Shirley's house, while Lloyd took the route to the city jail. Lloyd was nearly downtown when his cell phone rang. The caller ID showed his parents' phone number.

"Hi, Mom."

"Lloyd, what is going on in Houston?" his mother asked in a disturbed tone. "Your daddy and I have been watching the news here in Navasota, and it seems like all hell has broken loose."

"It has, Mama. This nonsense has everybody acting completely crazy. Mama, Ron was arrested."

"You have got to be kidding? Straight-laced Ron, who has never even had a ticket for jaywalking? How could anybody think that he had anything to do with the kidnapping?"

"That's just it, Mama. People aren't thinking; they are reacting emotionally. I think the police have arrested every black man in the city who owns a black SUV. It's going to take a while for the city to heal after all this is over."

"Are you one of the reporters on the story, Lloyd?"

"I'm actually the main reporter, Mama. I went to interview the woman whose baby was kidnapped, and she simply is not believable. But the police have accepted her story—hook, line and sinker. They are taking her description—if you can call it that—and are using the limited details she gave to try to catch the perpetrator. You should see the artist's sketch of the so-called kidnapper. It looks more like a cartoon character than an actual person."

"Lloyd, if you believe what she's saying is not true, you owe it to your newspaper and the citizens of Houston to uncover the truth. You know, the Bible says, 'The truth shall set you free.' If you find out the truth, the people of Houston will be set free from all this nonsense."

Whenever Lloyd's mother quoted scripture, he knew she was not in the mood to be challenged. "Right now, Mama, all I have is a hunch. I'll need a lot more than that to write something that my editor would even consider putting in the *Ledger*, let alone confront the police with my suspicions."

"You know I always say you should follow your first mind. That's what a hunch is, baby—your first mind. Lloyd, you didn't make it this far to walk away when you know a wrong has been done. I didn't raise you that way."

As always, she had worn him down, but he knew she was right. "Okay, Mama. Tomorrow morning I'll get started looking at this incident with a more critical eye. I'm sure Mrs. Pauley left some clues behind. People who believe they have committed the perfect crime usually get caught because they leave loose ends somewhere."

Lloyd had arrived at the downtown detention facility. "I'm pulling into the city jail parking lot now, Mama, so I'll call you later."

"Tell Ron we are praying for him."

"I will, Mama."

CHAPTER 14

Lloyd arrived at the city jail's intake area and showed his media credentials. With his media pass, he could get into a lot of places without being asked questions and the city jail was one of them.

"I'm Lloyd Palmer and I'm here to find out about the charges against Ron Singleton and the amount of his bond," Lloyd said to the policewoman at the intake desk. He knew that if bail was necessary, there were dozens of bail bondsmen's offices within a few blocks of the downtown lockup.

The policewoman checked the computer for the status of Ron's arrest. "Mr. Palmer, it appears that the charges against Mr. Singleton have been dropped, so he is free to go home. His alibi checked out, and the arresting officers decided not to pursue the resisting arrest charges. He's being processed now for release and should be out within the next thirty minutes. You can wait for him on that bench over there," she said, as she pointed to a wooden bench a few feet away.

"Thank you, officer. I'll wait."

Lloyd sat on the bench and immediately phoned Shirley, who answered on the first ring.

"Lloyd, are you there yet? Have you seen Ron?"

"Shirley, the charges against Ron have been dropped, and they're processing him for release right now. He should be home with you within an hour."

"Thank God, Lloyd. I was so worried about him. I can't tell you how much I appreciate you for doing this."

"Ron would do the same thing for me if the situations were reversed. I'm just glad he didn't have to stay here any longer than necessary. Tell Steph and Bria we both should be there soon."

"They're standing here next to me, and I'll be sure to tell them. See you soon."

Lloyd sat on the bench watching the steady stream of people inquiring about their family members or friends who had been arrested. The vast majority of them were black, and Lloyd wondered how many had been locked up because they drove the type of vehicle the police had been looking for. He felt guilty that he had played a role in the madness, however small his role may have been. Starting tomorrow morning, he was going to take matters into his own hands, no matter what Ed said.

The double doors at the end of the hallway opened and Ron walked through them in Lloyd's direction. Lloyd stood up to meet him and, as Ron approached him, Lloyd spread his arms to give him a hug.

"Glad to see you in one piece, man."

"It's good to be out, Lloyd. I never want to spend even five minutes behind bars again. I was getting claustrophobic in there. But the holding cell is full of brothas, some of whom were well dressed. I even saw another City of Houston employee from the Purchasing Department."

Lloyd and Ron began walking toward the exit. "If the cops don't solve this crime soon, there is going to be some sort of civil unrest. People are going to start taking matters into their own hands. There's only so much of this the community can take. Have they gotten any closer to finding the guy who kidnapped the Pauley baby?"

"That's just it, Ron. I think the whole thing is a fabrication, and I plan to prove it. I don't know what Mrs. Pauley's motivation is, but either she's hiding something, she has some type of mental disorder, or both. Black men just don't kidnap white babies. A purse snatching or carjacking, yes; a kidnapping, no way."

"If that's true, Lloyd, I'm not sure what's going to happen once the truth comes out. There'll be hell to pay."

CHAPTER 15

Once Lloyd had taken Ron home, he and Stephanie went home and went to bed. But Lloyd tossed and turned for several hours. His mind was still racing trying to figure out how he was going to approach peeling the layers away from Mrs. Pauley's story. He couldn't just go traipsing around the ritzy River Oaks community, door to door, and expect for the residents to open their doors to him. After all, a black man was suspected of committing a serious crime in their neighborhood. Their natural skepticism of any unfamiliar black male had now morphed into downright terror.

But he knew that someone in the neighborhood must have seen *something*. There had to be a way to get to the bottom of what really happened.

Then Lloyd had an idea. Maybe he could ask Charles to help him with some of the reporting. Lloyd didn't have any problem sharing the byline or the limelight once the crime was solved. With Charles' blonde good looks, he had front-door access to places Lloyd could not enter, even from the rear.

Lloyd also trusted Charles not to try to steal the story from him and call it his own. That had happened to Lloyd a couple of times, both at the *Ledger* and at other newspapers, until he found out that the competitive nature of most reporters meant that they couldn't be trusted. They'd stab their fellow reporters in the back and then consider it all part of the game. First thing in the morning, before he went into the office, Lloyd planned to call Charles' cell phone and map out a game plan.

After a night of restless sleep, Lloyd got up early the next morning, had a cup of coffee, and ate a quick breakfast. He waited until seven thirty, when he thought Charles would be awake, and called him on his cell phone.

"Hi, Lloyd," said Charles, sounding a bit groggy. "Why are you calling me so early? Is something wrong?"

"Charles, I'm calling about the River Oaks kidnapping story. The black community is up in arms about the police crackdown, and it won't be long before the anger reaches a boiling point. My best friend, Ron, was arrested last night, essentially because he was a black man driving a black SUV. This has gotten way out of control, and somebody needs to do something. I have reason to believe that Mrs. Pauley is making the whole thing up."

Charles had been sleepy up to that point, but after he heard Lloyd's accusation against Mrs. Pauley, he was wide awake. "Lloyd, I know you're upset, and I agree that the police are being overly aggressive. But why would Mrs. Pauley fabricate this? What would she have to gain?"

"I don't know, but I interviewed her yesterday, and there are a lot of inconsistencies with her account of what occurred."

"She's under a lot of stress. After all, her only child has been kidnapped. People under pressure will often misremember a detail or two. These things are usually cleared up as the police continue their investigation."

"That's just it, Charles, the police are not doing a very thorough job. They are basically taking Mrs. Pauley's word for everything that happened and are focusing their attention on capturing the perpetrator, rather than investigating the crime. I'm telling you that there's something fishy going on and I plan to get to the bottom of it. But I need your help."

"What do you want me to do, Lloyd?"

"I want to go to River Oaks and interview some of the neighbors. Maybe somebody saw something that will either confirm or cast doubt on Mrs. Pauley's story. But I need you to go with me to do the door knocking. You know how frightened some white people — especially women — can be when it comes to black men. Even with my media credentials, some of them simply will not open their front doors or drop their guard in my presence."

Charles frequently thought that Lloyd was overly paranoid when it came to dealings with white people. But he did want to be supportive. "I think you're way off base, Lloyd. But I agree that it's important to get this crime solved as soon as possible, so if you think a neighborhood canvas would help, then I'm in. I'm not sure the city can take much more of this stress without serious racial repercussions. We don't want a replay of the Los Angeles riots here in Houston."

Lloyd was relieved. "How soon can you be ready? I think it's best if we ride over there together."

"I'll be ready in thirty minutes," said Charles, as he got out of bed and headed toward the bathroom.

CHAPTER 16

Lloyd arrived at Charles' apartment within a few minutes and decided to park at the curbside and wait, rather than go inside. He called Charles' cell phone and when Charles answered said, "Hey man, I'm parked outside in front of your building. Are you ready?"

"I'll be down in a couple of minutes."

A few minutes later, Charles exited the building and got into Lloyd's car. "Okay, Lloyd, what's the game plan?"

Lloyd pulled the car away from the curb and headed in the direction of River Oaks. "I thought maybe you could interview some of the residents in close proximity to the Pauley home. They will be a lot more receptive to you asking them questions than they would if I was there."

"I don't think that's true, Lloyd. I think you're a bit too sensitive. You're a handsome, likeable guy and they won't tell me any more than they'd tell you."

Lloyd knew that Charles could be incredibly naïve, especially when racial matters were concerned. Charles believed everybody was like him—accepting people at face value without focusing on their ethnicity. But years of experienced had taught Lloyd that, when in doubt, most people subconsciously relied on racial stereotypes in the first few seconds of meeting people for the first time. For a lot of white people, that meant an abundance of caution was used when black men were in the vicinity.

"Trust me, Charles. If I had weeks to spend time with them and let them get to know me, I'm sure they would probably agree with you. But we don't have weeks or even days. This city is on edge and the tension is palpable. The first impression the folks in River Oaks will have of me will be that I'm someone to be feared, not trusted."

"I see how the women clutch their purses when I get into the elevator at work," Lloyd continued. "I'd probably have trouble catching a cab too, if Houston was a city where its residents used cab services. When I go out of town to New York or D.C., though, the cabs pass me by and pick up the next passenger a block past me, unless, of course, he happens to be a black man too."

"Okay, if you say so. What are you going to be doing while I'm going door to door hobnobbing with the wealthy socialites?" Charles asked sarcastically.

"I thought I'd talk to some of the groundskeepers who work outdoors. You know, the landscapers and even the folks who pick up the garbage. The hired help sometimes see things they don't mention, and they are usually invisible to those living the lifestyles of the rich and famous. They are very hesitant about going to the authorities, especially if they are challenging someone who is influential."

"I still think you're way off base, Lloyd. We should leave the detective work to the cops. But we both know reporters who've solved more than a crime or two, so I'm going mostly to support you in case you uncover something."

"I do appreciate you doing this for me, Charles, and I think you might be surprised at the results. Hey, we could become a famous two-man journalism team, like Woodward and Bernstein during the Watergate investigation," said Lloyd, only half jokingly.

Charles was still skeptical. "Let's see what happens before you break your arm patting yourself on the back," he replied as they approached one of the main streets leading into River Oaks. Since most of the homes were located on plots of an acre or more, the houses were far apart and there were only two or three on each side of the street per block. Lloyd and Charles thought their best bet was to speak to the neighbors in proximity to the Pauley home. When they turned onto Del Monte Drive, the street where the Pauleys lived, Lloyd pointed to the colonial style home directly across the street from their residence.

"Start with that one, Charles, and I'll walk around the block to see if any of the landscapers are outside."

Lloyd parked and they both exited the car, with Charles walking toward the house and Lloyd setting off on foot, thankful that it was springtime. The sweltering, humid Houston summers would have prohibited him from making his rounds in the neighborhood without breaking out into an almost immediate and continuous sweat.

He was careful to keep his leather-strapped portfolio in plain sight in case any policemen passed by. A black man on foot in River Oaks was inviting scrutiny, but he thought his suit and portfolio would at least not immediately label him a criminal. The powers that be in the River Oaks community hired police patrols to cruise the area every hour, and their presence had increased substantially since the kidnapping. If he was stopped by the cops, he'd just immediately flash his media card.

Meanwhile, Charles walked up to the front door of the mansion Lloyd had designated. There was a brass door knocker with the last name "Gerard" etched on it. Charles rang the doorbell. He waited a few seconds, and a silver-haired woman in a lavender maid's uniform opened the door. Charles flashed his award-winning smile and his press pass.

"Good morning, m'am. I was wondering if Mrs. Gerard is home. I'm Charles Scott with the *Houston Ledger*, and we're gathering information on the recent kidnapping of the Pauley baby. I'd like to ask her a few questions."

"My name is Helga," she said with what sounded like an Eastern European accent, maybe Russian or German. "Please come in, sir. I'll get her." She directed Charles inside and motioned for him to wait in the foyer.

As Charles waited, he took in the breathtaking surroundings. The marble stairway cascaded to the second floor, and the three-tier crystal chandelier hanging from the vaulted ceiling was the largest one he had ever seen.

There were vases and artwork, obviously priceless, strategically positioned throughout the foyer area. He'd only been inside a handful of River Oaks homes, and each experience revealed the stark difference between the relatively meager dwellings of regular folks and the lavish trappings possessed by the well-to-do.

Mrs. Gerard gracefully descended the stairs and, even though it was rather early in the morning, she was already fully dressed in classic business attire. She obviously had plans to go out for the day. Her demeanor and wardrobe were that of a middle-aged woman, but Charles noticed very few facial wrinkles. His guess was that, like so many wealthy women, she'd had some plastic surgery or enhancements done. Once she reached the bottom of the stairs, she extended her hand and shook Charles'.

"Welcome to my home, Mr. Scott. As I told the police, I don't have any information regarding the kidnapping. The morning the Pauley baby was taken was the day I usually volunteer at the Museum of Fine Arts, and I was there most of the day."

Charles thought quickly and decided to pivot from his original game plan. "Mrs. Gerard, I'm actually working on a different aspect of the story. We also want to report on the Pauley family and their stature within the Houston social and civic community."

"Now is obviously not a good time to question Mrs. Pauley about her social activities," added Charles, "so we thought we would interview a few of her neighbors and friends to get their insights. Would you mind speaking with me for a few minutes?"

"Of course not. Let's go sit in the family room," she said, as she turned to the north side of the mansion and strolled—practically glided—toward the room where they would spend the next few minutes. Mrs. Gerard exuded the aura of old money. "Would you like some coffee or tea, Mr. Scott?"

"Call me Charles, please. As a matter of fact, I'd love some coffee. I take it black."

As they entered the den, Mrs. Gerard used the wall intercom to give Helga instructions regarding their refreshments. She then went over to the love seat and sat down. "Please sit there, Charles," she said, as she extended her hand and directed him to the matching love seat facing her. An antique coffee table separated them.

"I won't take up a lot of your time, Mrs. Gerard. I just have a few questions. How long have you known Mrs. Pauley?"

"I believe the Pauleys moved into the neighborhood about five years ago. Her husband has a successful oil and gas business and travels a lot. She's from a small town somewhere in the Midwest. Definitely new money."

Charles smiled. He'd heard that the wealthy often distinguished between those they considered the Blue Bloods, with multi-generational property and status, versus the Nouveau Riche, whose parents were usually poor or middle-class and who tended to flaunt their wealth with ostentatious trappings and bling. He'd just never met anyone face to face who had made the comparison. To him, they all had more money than he could imagine in his lifetime, so what difference did it make?

Helga entered the room carrying a silver tray with an accompanying silver coffee service. "Will there be anything else, Mrs. Gerard?" she said as she set the tray on the coffee table.

"Thank you, Helga. No, that will be all."

The silence hung in the air during the few seconds it took Helga to leave the room.

"As I was saying, Mrs. Gerard, I'd like to ask you a few questions about Mrs. Pauley. Do you know if she has any hobbies? What does she do in her spare time, and who are some of her close friends?"

"We didn't exactly run in the same circles, you understand. I spend a lot of time with my volunteer work and raising funds for the underprivileged. We are also very involved with the annual Houston Livestock and Rodeo Show and, of course, with local and state politics. I've been state chairwoman of the Republican Women of Texas for the past five years," she added, while Charles listened intently as she rattled off her list of bona fides.

"But I believe Mrs. Pauley was a little bit lonely."

"Why do you say that?" Charles asked as he straightened up and leaned closer towards her.

"Well, a couple of times she came over for tea. I don't think her husband likes her to entertain friends at their home. He seems to be very possessive, wants to keep her all to himself."

"She told me she spends a lot of time on the Internet. She had some problems with her pregnancy when she was carrying little Hunter and was on bed rest for the last trimester, so I suppose surfing the Internet kept her from going stir crazy."

"Once the baby came, I thought she would perk up a bit, but she didn't. Most of the new mothers I know are quite pleased with their babies, but she seemed to be a little down after the baby was born."

"Are you saying that you think she suffers from post-partum depression?" Charles picked up the coffee cup and sipped some of the coffee but never took his eyes off Mrs. Gerard.

"I'm no psychiatrist, but having three children of my own, I remember how ecstatic I was after each of their births. She mentioned something to me a couple of weeks ago about the burdens of motherhood. I thought it was odd that she would use the term 'burdens.' Odd indeed."

"You said that Mrs. Pauley spends a lot of time on the Internet. Did she talk to you about some of the web sites she visited? Do you know whether or not she was meeting people online?"

"It's none of my business, Charles. Adults can do as they please. But she did mention that she visited some online gambling sites—vegasgambling.com or something like that. People will do all sorts of things, especially when they are bored."

"Online gambling sites. That's very interesting, Mrs. Gerard. Were you ever with her when she visited these web sites?"

"Oh, goodness no. I've never been to her home. Most of my friends are members of the River Oaks Country Club, and we get together to play bridge or have cocktails. I invited her here a few times strictly as a courtesy, to be neighborly," she said, as if admitting a close relationship with Mrs. Pauley would somehow tarnish her credentials among the elite. "As I said, we don't run in the same circles. She mentioned the gambling merely in passing. Could that be important to your story?"

"I'm not sure, Mrs. Gerard, but I appreciate your hospitality and your candor."

"I'd appreciate it if you wouldn't use my name when you write your story, Charles. Mr. Gerard and I try to keep our names out of the papers, except in the Society and Lifestyle sections, of course."

"Don't worry, Mrs. Gerard. I may not even need to use the details you've given me. But, if I do, I'll use very general terms like 'River Oaks residents said,' or something to that effect. I keep all of my sources strictly confidential."

Charles rose from his seat to leave. "Thank you for inviting me into your home, and I hope I haven't kept you from anything."

"Not at all. The pleasure has been all mine. I still have plenty of time to get to my weekly bridge game at the Country Club. Helga will show you out."

Helga appeared in the family room doorway, as if on cue.

As Charles went to the front door and walked out onto the porch, he reached into his shirt pocket to retrieve his cell phone. For the first time since he'd heard about the Pauley kidnapping, Charles had a sneaking suspicion that Lloyd might be right. Something was fishy about this whole thing and, as he dialed Lloyd's number, he hoped the two of them could get to the bottom of it.

CHAPTER 17

When Lloyd rounded the corner from the Gerard mansion, he walked about a block before he saw a landscaper planting begonias in the front flower bed of the home across the street. Since he wasn't far from the Gerard home, Lloyd thought perhaps the landscaper had seen something on the day of the kidnapping. It was about the same time of the day that Mrs. Pauley said her baby had been snatched.

Lloyd knew that most of the landscapers in Houston were Mexican immigrants, some in the country illegally. They tended to shy away from the authorities for fear of being deported or, if here legally, for fear of putting some of their family members with questionable citizenship documents in jeopardy.

Lloyd hoped the yardman had a green card and that his English was good enough for them to communicate adequately. He had always wanted to pick up a bit of the Spanish language but just had never gotten around to it. He didn't want to have to use sign language to try to decipher whatever was said.

Lloyd walked toward the landscaper and called to him, "Excuse me, sir, I'm with the *Houston Ledger*. May I speak with you for a moment?"

"Senor, I am working and cannot talk right now," said the landscaper, as he spoke haltingly but with apparently decent English skills.

"Oh, it will only take a few minutes. I'm working on a story about the Pauley kidnapping and just wanted to ask you a couple of questions."

"Well, okay, but do it fast. Mrs. Parker wants to get these flowers planted in her front yard before noon."

Lloyd assumed that Mrs. Parker was the owner of the home in whose yard the landscaper was working. "What's your name?"

"My name is José, Senor."

"José, were you working outside in this same area yesterday morning?"

"Yes, sir. I always get an early start at about seven o'clock before it gets too hot outside."

"Do you know Mrs. Pauley, the lady who lives in that house?" said Lloyd, as he pointed to the Pauley home down the street.

"I have never spoken to her, Senor, but I know what she looks like."

"Did you see her yesterday?"

"Yes. She walks through the neighborhood with her stroller some mornings. She usually goes in the other direction, but yesterday she walked the stroller past Mrs. Parker's house and went toward those trees over there," said José, as he pointed to a clump of trees about one hundred yards east of the Parker home.

"About what time was that, José?"

"I'm not sure, Senor, but I was outside a couple of hours when I saw her, so it had to be about nine o'clock."

"Did she see you?"

"I don't think so because she did not look in my direction. She was looking straight ahead."

"Did you see what she did once she went over to the clump of trees?"

"I really wasn't paying close attention, Senor, but I did notice something when she walked the stroller back this way."

"What was that, José?"

"The stroller was empty. The baby was in the stroller when she went over to the trees, but he wasn't in there when she came back."

"Are you sure about that, José?"

"Yes. I remember it because I thought it was very strange. But I thought maybe she took the baby over to a neighbor's house over that way, and the neighbor was watching the baby for her. Then I thought to myself, 'Why didn't she leave the stroller there so she wouldn't have to bring it back again?'"

"Did you know about the kidnapping, José? Why didn't you report this to the police?"

"Senor, I work from seven in the morning to about eight at night. When I get home I don't watch the news very much. We have our family meal, and it's almost time for bed."

"Haven't you seen the police cars everywhere? Didn't you suspect that a crime had been committed?"

"I've seen the cars, Senor, but my green card expired a couple of months ago and I don't want any trouble. I have a wife and five children to support. Senor, please don't say anything about me to the police."

"Don't worry, José, your secret is safe with me. But I appreciate the information you've given me. It might be helpful in solving the crime."

"If it's all right with you, Senor, I need to get back to my work."

"Of course, thank you again, José," Lloyd said as he shook the landscaper's hand. José then went back to the flower bed and started shoveling dark mulch around the begonias.

Lloyd could not believe what he had heard. It looked as though Mrs. Pauley had indeed killed her baby, and the poor child's remains were probably buried in the soil at the base of that clump of trees. *Does your newspaper sometimes print information in stories that later turns out to be false?* Hamisi's words echoed in his mind, penetrating Lloyd's soul with such intensity that he became dizzy.

His cell phone rang, breaking the temporary trance, and he pulled it out of his pocket. It was Charles.

"Charles, have you finished interviewing the lady at the house I sent you to?"

"Yes, her name is Mrs. Gerard and she had some very interesting things to say about Mrs. Pauley. What did you find out?"

"We may have solved this crime, Charles. I need you to walk a couple of blocks to the east and meet me on the corner of Del Monte Drive and River Oaks Boulevard. Prepare yourself for what could be a gruesome discovery."

CHAPTER 18

Lloyd waited for Charles at the corner of River Oaks Boulevard as he contemplated their next move. He knew it would probably be best to contact the police, give them his information, and have them investigate the crime scene. If he and Charles unearthed what Lloyd felt sure would be the remains of the unfortunate Pauley baby, they could contaminate some of the evidence.

But Lloyd did not trust the police to charge Mrs. Pauley with the murder, nor did he trust the Harris County District Attorney to vigorously prosecute the case. The rich often got away with murder, but with Mrs. Pauley casting the long shadow of the law on all of the city's black males, he was determined not to let her off the hook. If he brought the evidence to the authorities himself, they might even try to accuse him of being the guilty party. Having Charles with him as a corroborating witness was the best way to hedge his bets.

He saw Charles approaching from a block away. "It's a good thing you have on casual shoes because you may have to get a little dirt on them before we're done here."

"Lloyd, what are you talking about? Did one of the landscapers see something?"

"He may have seen the crime in progress, but we'll have to do a little digging to be sure."

"Do you mean we need to interview some more people?"

"No, Charles. Actual digging, as in removing earth. I spoke to the landscaper over there whose name is José. His green card expired; so he wouldn't go on the record with his statement, and I told him I would protect his identity. He says he saw Mrs. Pauley carry the stroller toward that clump of trees over there and when she returned there was no baby in the stroller. I'll bet you a hundred dollars that she buried the baby over there and then pretended he was kidnapped."

Charles was incredulous. "Lloyd, why would she do something as monstrous as that? Mrs. Gerard said that Mrs. Pauley seemed a little depressed, but to kill her own baby? That's horrible, just horrible."

"I've heard about women who have babies and can't cope with the pressure and the demands that a newborn requires," Lloyd replied. "I believe the experts call it post-partum depression. Do you remember that case several years ago where a woman here in Houston drowned all five of her children in the bathtub because of depression?"

"Yes, I think her name was Andrea Yates. Even the news reporters covering that story were shocked by that one, and you know from experience that guys in our profession see all kinds of horrifying cases."

"A lot of people have a hard time accepting the fact that wealthy people can have serious mental problems that have not been treated. But I know that no black man in this city kidnapped that baby, and the evidence is right over there," Lloyd said as he pointed to the clump of trees José identified. "I want you to go with me to dig up the area under those trees and see what we find."

"Mrs. Gerard did say something about a potential gambling problem the Pauley woman may have. I wonder if the two—the depression and the gambling—are somehow connected? But, Lloyd, shouldn't we call the police first? I know they would want to keep the crime scene intact."

"I'm not going to wait around for the police and the rest of the authorities in this town to cover up this crime. They are going to bend over backwards to pin this on the first black male they find who most closely fits the description. Can you imagine the repercussions if the police have to admit that they failed to investigate this crime?"

Lloyd was ready to do whatever needed to be done. He just had to convince Charles. "You've come with me this far, Charles, and since I first interviewed Mrs. Pauley I've been right about my suspicions. I'm asking you to help me solve this crime and heal this city. Will you help me?"

Charles closed his eyes and rubbed his temples, trying to decide what to do. He knew he should follow the normal protocol, contact the authorities, and wait for them to uncover the evidence. And he thought Lloyd was way too paranoid.

But he admitted that he was clueless about what it felt like to be a black man in America. To him, Lloyd was no different than his other friends. Other than their contrasting tastes in music and food, they shared a lot of the same interests and always got along. He counted Lloyd among his closest friends and rarely even thought about the fact that he was black.

But Charles knew his attitudes were not shared by everyone. He had been at more than one party where no black people were present, and someone told a "black joke" that made everyone within earshot double over with laughter.

Today, Charles saw his friend come alive as a journalist. Lloyd was usually very cautious and laid back, but working on this story had imbued him with an energy and determination Charles hadn't seen before. He owed it to him to take things one step further.

And, besides, there could be an upside professionally. If Lloyd's suspicions were correct, he'd share the byline on the city's biggest news story of the decade.

"Okay, Lloyd, let's go," Charles said, as they headed across the lawn to what looked like a cluster of crepe myrtle trees. They both sensed that a life altering future might lie before them.

CHAPTER 19

Eight crepe myrtle trees stood clustered together in groups of two each. A wooden bench graced each side of the mini park and a variety of colorful seasonal flowers were planted there as well. The soft chirping of birds and a gentle breeze blowing from the north contrasted with the sense of doom Lloyd and Charles felt as they cautiously approached the area and looked around.

"I'm no detective, Lloyd, so what do you think we should be looking for?" asked Charles.

"Well, if Mrs. Pauley buried her baby in the earth beneath these trees, there should be some soil that looks as though it has recently been displaced. It would look different than the soil around it. That's what we should be looking for."

They examined the area closest to them, careful to keep their feet on the grass and not breach the flower bed itself, but they saw nothing unusual.

"You go that way," said Lloyd, as he pointed Charles to the right while he walked to the left himself. "She would probably have done it in the area behind the trees so it wouldn't be so obvious. Afterwards, if there was a hard rain, the soil would settle and there would be no signs whatsoever that anyone had been digging here."

Lloyd mentally divided the area into four quadrants, focusing first on the area beneath the park bench, then the front of the tree closest to him, then the left and, finally, the right. He was looking for anything that seemed out of place.

"Do you see anything, Charles?"

"No. I'm not even sure what I'm looking for. This could be a complete waste of time, you know."

"If you really thought that, you wouldn't be here," said Lloyd, as he continued to scan his side of the mini-park and then noticed four smooth, flat stones beneath the trees that did not have a companion set on the other side. He looked back and forth, matching items on both sides. Yes, there was a park bench here, and there. There were the same number of trees planted an equal distance apart, and each of the flower clusters had nearly the identical number of flowers and were an equal distance apart.

The stones did not belong in that formation. This could be the place.

"Charles, come here and take a look at these stones."

Charles walked toward Lloyd and noticed the stones as well. Lloyd took a deep breath. "I think this is it, Charles. I think this is where Mrs. Pauley buried her baby. Let's move the stones and see if something is down there."

"Lloyd, we could completely contaminate the crime scene. What if there are fingerprints on the stones? Shouldn't we call the police now and wait?"

Lloyd thought a minute. Charles could be right about the fingerprints. "There's no way that I'm turning back now, Charles. But you're right about the fingerprints. I think I have some tissues in my brief bag, and I'll use those to make sure I don't smear any prints that are already there."

Lloyd took his bag off his shoulder and pulled out his travel-sized package of tissues. Stephanie had loaded up his bag with the tissues and other things she thought he might need: a package of Advil, lotion, band-aids, hand sanitizer. Lloyd had thought she was being too much of a mother hen, but now he was grateful for her attention to detail.

"Okay, here goes," said Lloyd, as he carefully stepped toward the trees and knelt down on the grassy area beneath. He used the tissue to remove the stones one by one.

Then he reached into his pocket and pulled out his cash clamped with a money clip. The money clip would make a good digging tool. He began to dig, meticulously removing about a tablespoon of dark mulch each time until he arrived at the soil below.

Lloyd used the same technique as he removed soil bit by bit. His heart was pounding fast—he really did not want to uncover what he thought could be a few inches below him.

"Do you see anything yet?" whispered Charles.

"Not yet, but I need you to be quiet. I'm trying to concentrate, and I don't want to disturb more of the area than necessary."

Lloyd continued the painstaking task of the dreaded exhumation as beads of sweat began to form on his brow. Then, as he removed another clump of soil, he saw a piece of light blue flannel, what could have been part of a baby blanket.

"Oh my God, Charles, I think I found him," he said, as Charles moved closer to him and kneeled down beside him. Lloyd stopped digging, almost afraid to continue.

"You've got to keep going, Lloyd. We've got to be sure."

Lloyd removed more dirt, and the flannel blanket was now in plain view. When he removed the next clump of dirt, he uncovered a small, pale baby's hand. Lloyd could go no further and he jumped up, ran toward the adjacent shrubs and retched until his morning breakfast and anything else that his stomach contained was completely expelled. They had found him. They had found little Hunter Pauley.

CHAPTER 20

For a few moments, Lloyd and Charles were both stunned, paralyzed where they stood and unable to move or think. They were trying to wrap their minds around what had just happened and forget that there was a small corpse buried just inches away. The gravity of their discovery was starting to sink in. Gradually, they shook themselves out of their stupor, breathed deeply and looked at each other.

Lloyd, still a bit queasy, said, "Charles. We need to call Ed and then call the police."

Ed insisted on being the first one notified of a major breaking story and would give them instructions on how to proceed. He'd also assign a photographer to come out and chronicle images of the crime scene and, once the police arrived, Mrs. Pauley's arrest. Lloyd wasn't sure which one of them should make the phone call.

"Charles, maybe you should call Ed. He probably won't believe what I tell him, and we need to get the police out here immediately."

"Lloyd, this is your story. You uncovered it and you should take the full credit. Besides," he said jokingly, "Ed will probably flip his lid when you break the news to him, and I'd like to be a fly on the wall to see his reaction. Now is as good a time as any for you to confront him. It's long overdue."

Lloyd still had reservations. "Okay, man, here goes," he said, as he pressed the touch screen on his cell phone and placed the call. When Ed answered, Lloyd hesitated at first, then found his voice.

"Ed, this is Lloyd. Charles and I just found some evidence that solves the Pauley kidnapping. The *Ledger* will have an exclusive on this one."

"That's great. So the cops found the guy who did it, huh? Did he still have the kid with him?"

"No, that's just it, Ed. There was no guy. Mrs. Pauley faked the whole thing. She killed her baby and buried him in a park not far from their home."

"That makes no sense at all, Lloyd. After ten years with the *Ledger* you still haven't learned not to believe every cock-in-bull story somebody tells you? One of the other reporters told me your best friend got locked up last night for the kidnapping and was later released. Is this some sort of vendetta to get back at the police?"

Listening to Ed's diatribe, Lloyd first rolled his eyes. Then he was fuming. "Listen, Ed. Charles and I found the baby's body. We wanted to call you first before we called the police. Do you want to send out a photographer or not?"

There was silence on the phone. Ed was speechless, a rarity indeed. But his temporary silence quickly subsided. "Let me speak with Charles."

"Sure, Ed." Lloyd handed Charles the phone. "He wants to speak with you."

Charles took the phone. "Ed, you are wasting precious time. "If you want the *Ledger* to get credit for breaking this story, you need to act now."

"Is Lloyd telling the truth? You two found the Pauley baby's body?"

"Of course he's telling the truth, Ed. You need to get our best people on this one. I think you should send Patty and Jerry out here, if they are available. They are our two best photographers."

Ed collected himself. "Okay, wait ten minutes and then call the police. I want to make sure Patty and Jerry are at least on their way before the cops get there. And the TV stations listen to the police scanners, so we want to get all of our preliminary work done before they get the camera trucks out there."

Then Ed went into overdrive. "Stay right where you are; protect the crime scene. We don't want any busy bodies wandering around, and we can't forget the possibility of stray animals passing by. We have to work all of the angles. Charles, have you interviewed any of the neighbors?"

"Yes, we interviewed Mrs. Girard who lives close by. She hinted that Mrs. Pauley may be suffering from post-partum depression. She also thought there might be a gambling problem. Mrs. Girard mentioned something about gambling web sites Mrs. Pauley frequently visited."

"Okay, Charles. I know a computer hacker who may be able to get into Mrs. Pauley's computer before the cops get there and copy it. He can download her online activity and we can sift through it here. Good work."

Charles responded, "Ed, the credit really belongs to Lloyd . . ." But Ed had already hung up the phone.

"Well, what did he say?" asked Lloyd.

"He wants us to wait here for ten minutes before calling the police. He's getting our best people on it and Patty and Jerry should be here soon."

"How did he sound?"

"Once he realized we were telling the truth, he was back to his old self. You know, Ed lives for days like this when the *Ledger* can break a major story. It just worked out completely different than he thought, but selling newspapers is what gets his juices flowing."

"What did he say about the gambling angle?"

"He says he knows a computer hacker who should be able to get into Mrs. Pauley's computer before the police arrive and download her online activity. People don't realize how easy it is for a good computer hacker to get into their computer hard drives remotely."

"Well, I don't mind waiting here for a few minutes. I'd actually like to sit down for a few minutes and collect my thoughts. Let's sit on this bench," Lloyd said, as he pointed to one of the wooden benches and walked over to it. Charles followed.

"We can also watch the street from here and make sure Mrs. Pauley doesn't leave her home. But I don't ever want to look at Hunter Pauley's body again."

CHAPTER 21

Two police cars arrived at the mini park within a few minutes after Lloyd and Charles called. There were still police officers stationed at the Pauley home, who had set up recording equipment in the event the kidnappers called to demand a ransom payment in exchange for Hunter. No one had called and now the reason was clear: The kidnappers didn't exist.

Lloyd gave the police officers Jose's account of what happened, honoring the gardener's request that his identity remain a secret. The officers were skeptical at first, and they weren't particularly happy about the crime scene being disturbed. But once Hunter Pauley's body was uncovered and his remains transferred to the awaiting coroner's station wagon, they went to the Pauley residence and took Mrs. Pauley in for questioning.

The damage Mrs. Pauley caused, however, extended well beyond the death of her two-month-old son. Not only had she killed her own baby, but she had shattered the usually harmonious relationship between the city government and the black community.

Lloyd and Charles headed back to the office to file their story for the *Ledger*'s afternoon online edition. When they arrived, they went to Ed's office to brief him about the morning's developments. Ed was on the phone wrapping up a call when they walked in, and he hung up shortly after they sat down in the two chairs facing his desk.

"Hi guys. That was my computer expert on the phone. He's already hacked into Mrs. Pauley's home computer. And you won't believe what he found!"

Ed didn't wait for them to respond and kept going. "Mrs. Pauley regularly visited several online gambling sites and owed nearly a million dollars in gambling debts. That might have something to do with why she faked the kidnapping, but we'll see once the police uncover more evidence."

"Charles, I want to congratulate you on a job well done," Ed continued, assuming that Charles had been the one who broke the story. "We've got media from all over the country calling the *Ledger* for details. CNN and MSNBC both want you to appear on the network this evening as the lead reporter. I've already told them you would do it."

Lloyd and Charles looked at each other and then back at Ed. Charles spoke first, "Uh, Ed. You've got the whole thing backwards."

"What do you mean?" asked Ed.

"It was Lloyd who broke this story. He interviewed Mrs. Pauley yesterday and was suspicious about her responses to his questions. I was extremely skeptical when he told me about it and thought he was being paranoid, but I reluctantly agreed to go along with him this morning to investigate further. If it wasn't for Lloyd, both this newspaper and the police would still be chasing their tails looking for a phantom kidnapper."

"You've got to be kidding. I don't believe it," Ed replied incredulously, speaking directly to Charles as if Lloyd were invisible.

"Believe it," said Charles. "I am not going to help you take this accomplishment away from him. He deserves a medal for what he's done and, quite frankly, you owe him an apology."

Ed looked at Charles, then at Lloyd. His entire demeanor had changed from recalcitrant to amenable. "Well, Lloyd, is this true?"

"Yes, it is Ed. I mentioned to you yesterday that I thought the whole Pauley thing was a hoax, but you refused to listen. Now, besides preparing the reports for this afternoon's paper, we've got a much more serious problem on our hands."

"What do you mean?" asked Ed.

"The black community has been under siege since this whole kidnapping fiasco started. Once the word spreads that the whole thing was one big con, the people are going to be outraged. Because of the *Ledger*'s complicit role in this, there will probably be pickets and protests for weeks. The circulation boost the paper gains from reporting the story will likely be offset by the subscription cancellations from your black readers."

From the expression on Ed's face, it was obvious he had focused solely on the *Ledger*'s national exposure for breaking the story and hadn't thought about community reaction at all. This could be a colossal problem for the newspaper and for the political establishment. "You could be right, Lloyd. What should we do?"

"So now you're asking for my advice? That's a first."

"The sarcasm isn't necessary. I'll admit that perhaps I should have listened and been a little more objective about the Pauley kidnapping. But you always walk around here with such a chip on your shoulder, I just thought it was more of the same racial sensitivity I see from you all the time."

Lloyd was boiling inside now, about to explode. "You're going to sit there and accuse me of racial sensitivity?"

"After the rush to judgment from you and the entire police force who would rather believe a black man—any black man—was guilty than scrutinize the obvious flaws in Mrs. Pauley's story? Then you assumed Charles broke the story when he wouldn't have even known about it if I hadn't called him this morning."

Charles contemplated interjecting into the conversation to try and lower the emotional volume, but decided against it. If Lloyd needed him to get involved, he would let him know.

While Lloyd unleashed his anger, Ed's mind was racing, as he thought about a strategy to deal with the black community. He had to figure out a way to persuade Lloyd to cooperate with the paper's efforts to salvage its reputation. Ed realized he needed Lloyd as the spokesperson to report the story. This bitter pill would go down a lot easier in the black community if a black reporter delivered the news.

"Slow down, Lloyd. I admit I made a mistake, okay? I'd like you to do the interviews with CNN and MSNBC, but I don't have a clue how to handle the folks in the Third and Fifth Wards. What would you recommend we do?"

Lloyd wasn't expecting Ed to concede so easily, but there was no way he was going to publicly take the flack for the *Ledger*'s blunder. If he did, he might as well leave town for good.

He would be like Christopher Darden, the black prosecutor who tried to convict O. J. Simpson—a traitor, despised by the black community for the next twenty years. But he could use this as an opportunity to force the *Ledger* to stop treating its black citizens as one-dimensional beings in its news reports, seen only through the prism of dysfunction or acrimony.

"Okay, Ed. I'm willing to do the interviews and help you run interference with the black community, on one condition."

"What's that?"

"That everything is done on my terms. First, when I do the interviews, I will be free to answer all questions truthfully. That means that if they ask me if the newspaper got it wrong initially, then my emphatic answer would be 'yes.'"

"I'm not going to agree to have you publicly air a personal vendetta with the newspaper," replied Ed.

"Ed, I'm a professional. Don't worry, I'm not going to make any statements that would make the *Ledger* liable for damages. Besides, you can check with our attorneys, but since we didn't actually name anyone as a suspect, it would be difficult for us to be sued for any actions the police took in investigating the crime."

"Is there anything else?"

"Yes, there's plenty. The *Ledger* needs to print a full-page, public apology on the back page of the front section of the newspaper, to run in tomorrow's edition. Then, we need to have a team of representatives from the newspaper to go to the church meetings tonight and the rest of this week to apologize personally to the congregations and others who attend."

"What church meetings? And how are we going to cover that much ground? We only have a few black employees."

"Ed, once this story breaks, most of the large black churches in town are going to have mass meetings to discuss the community's response. They won't waste any time, and the meetings will probably start tonight and take place throughout the week.

"But the black employees aren't the ones who need to go to the churches," Lloyd continued. "It should be some of the paper's top level editors and executives. The black employees didn't make any of the decisions that led to the rush to judgment about the Pauley kidnapping. The paper can't hide behind them to soften the blow of the community's outrage.

"The important thing is that we get out front of this before it snowballs," he added. "We need to extinguish the emotional fires before the Nation of Islam, the New Black Panther Party and the other grass roots groups organize and make this a four-week nightmare. Otherwise, the *Ledger* will be the lead story on every news network for the next thirty days, and it won't be for anything remotely positive."

Lloyd knew he had Ed over a barrel and it felt great. Ed had never given Lloyd credit for his reporting skills or his intellect. He had used intimidation tactics to keep Lloyd from pursuing advancement, to keep him in fear of losing his job if he pushed the envelope too much. Now the tables were turned.

Ed was reluctant, but knew he had no choice. He'd have to get Seymour Johnson, the president of the *Ledger*, involved, especially if they were going to send some of the bigwigs to the churches.

"Okay, I'll call Mr. Johnson's office and see who he wants to call on to represent us at those meetings tonight. The CNN and MSNBC interviews are scheduled for three o'clock this afternoon, so you and Charles need to get finished with today's story by then. They'll be interviewing you on a satellite feed from the news room."

"Okay, Ed."

"And another thing. You'll need to work with the folks in layout and advertising for the wording of that full-page ad. I need to approve it before it goes to press, but you'll need to set it up. Make sure we hit all of the relevant points. And, Lloyd?"

"Yes, Ed?"

"This had better work. There's a lot riding on this."

Lloyd sensed that Ed was trying to shift the blame to him and he wanted to make it clear where the responsibility lay. "Ed, I am giving you suggestions based on my personal experience and knowledge about the black community. But, as a reporter, I fulfilled my responsibility when I tried to warn you not to run with the erroneous story. If this effort to mend fences with the black community doesn't succeed, it won't be my fault. It will be yours."

Ed couldn't believe Lloyd was issuing ultimatums. Once this crisis was over, he'd have to deal with him. He couldn't afford to tolerate insubordination from his reporters, especially his affirmative action hires.

"That will be all, for now," said Ed.

As Lloyd and Charles, both with smiles on their faces, left the office, Lloyd felt like a new man, finally getting the recognition he'd yearned for so long. Charles was proud of his friend and equally pleased with the small role he had played in breaking the story. But Ed was not smiling at all. He didn't like having his nuts in a vise, and that's the position Lloyd had forced him into. If Lloyd pushed his demands further, Ed would have to do something about it.

CHAPTER 22

Lloyd's plan unfolded and things went surprisingly well. The church meetings were packed to capacity with standing room only crowds. The *Ledger* executives spoke to the audiences, did a complete and unequivocal mea culpa, and apologized for any pain the paper had caused the black community with its news reports.

The Chief of Police also made his rounds that night, assuring the citizens that all of those who had been falsely arrested would receive a $1,000 check from the city of Houston as compensation. The City Council had called an emergency session that afternoon to allocate the funds.

Lloyd was interviewed on the national news programs on all of the major networks and cable news channels. After Lloyd's TV appearances and the news circulated about the actions the city had taken, rather than having a blemished reputation, Houston was being hailed as a model for other cities on how to respond when racial tensions flair.

Mrs. Pauley was arrested and charged with first-degree capital murder. Further investigation revealed that she had purchased a $2 million insurance policy on Hunter — an unusually large sum for an infant. Apparently, she had planned to use the insurance proceeds to pay off her gambling debts.

Her husband traveled constantly and spent more time away from home than he did in Houston, so he was unaware of the insurance policy or his wife's bout of post-partum depression. He was brought to the police station for questioning but was cleared of all charges. Mrs. Pauley's attorney entered a plea of not guilty by reason of mental defect, citing her post-partum depression as an extenuating factor.

After filing the last installment of his news report that evening, Lloyd went home physically and emotionally exhausted. He wasn't sure whether or not there would be any repercussions from his confrontation with Ed, and, frankly, he didn't care. He was fed up with Ed's tirades and mood swings, and he decided that night that he wasn't going to take it anymore. If it cost him his job, so be it.

The exposure he had received as a result of breaking the Pauley story had raised his profile and his value in the journalism profession. He'd already received two text messages from colleagues in other states, asking him if he'd consider leaving the *Ledger* to work at regional or national publications. Thanks to his mother's prodding, he no longer had to live in fear that losing his job at the *Ledger* would be the end of the world.

He couldn't wait to get home to Stephanie's cooking and, later on, the release of all of his pent-up tension once they went to bed. Stephanie had a prim-and-proper public persona, but she had a sexual appetite that sometimes surpassed his. She had lots of tricks up her sleeve and, when Bria wasn't home, she had once greeted him at the door completely nude except for the red silk and lace thong she wore. That wild night of passion was irrevocably etched in his mind, and he would summon it often at will.

On the way home, his cell phone rang. Lloyd looked at the display and saw it was an incoming call from his best friend, Ron. "Hey, Ron. I'm on my way home. Sorry I haven't had a chance to call you today, but I've been tied up with this story."

"No need to apologize, Lloyd. I've been watching the news all day, and I almost had to do a double take. I'm used to seeing my bashful best friend shy away from the cameras, but you were handling everything like an old pro."

"It's been a trial by fire, Ron, almost like an out-of-body experience. I still can't believe it's happened. When I dug that poor Pauley baby out of the shallow grave, I thought I was going to pass out. I can't believe someone would do that to her own baby."

"I would have passed out too or, on second thought, I would have never been there in the first place. That was a really brave thing you did, Lloyd, and the city owes you a big one. I hope you figure out a way to cash in."

"I've been thinking about ways for this to advance my career. This may be my only shot out of this holding pattern I've been in. I'll let you know before I make any major moves, okay?"

"You'd better. Don't forget about us little people once you hit the big time," Ron said jokingly, and they both laughed.

"I'm pulling up to the house now, and I'm ready to eat and go to bed. I'm really tired, so I'll give you a call tomorrow."

"That's cool. Later, man."

Lloyd hung up and got out of his car. When he opened the door to his house, he heard the television playing in the den. Stephanie had finished cooking dinner hours ago, since it was past nine o'clock when he got there. When he entered the room, she was seated on the love seat watching one of her favorite programs.

"Hi, honey, have you been watching the news?" he asked.

"Of course. I've been channel surfing so I could watch you on all the networks. You're a regular celebrity," she said and broke out in a wide grin.

"Hardly. But my advice seems to have helped the paper navigate this crisis. Ed's running a full-page ad tomorrow apologizing for any pain caused to the black community from our reporting. But, I doubt this attitude of inclusiveness will last. Things will be back to normal in a week or two with black criminals once again gracing the *Ledger*'s front page. Otherwise, we don't exist as far as the paper is concerned."

"You never know, Lloyd. It could get better. Maybe Ed has learned something from this incident."

"He may have learned something, but that doesn't mean he's going to change. Ed's a good old boy from way back. It's hard to teach an old dog any new tricks. By the way, where's Bria?"

"She had an exhausting day at cheerleading practice and decided to go to bed early. Oh, I almost forgot, Lloyd. You got a call earlier tonight."

"From who?"

"He had an African accent and he said his name was Hamisi. Isn't that the man you said you were doing research on?"

Lloyd was both pleased and surprised, since the last thing he expected was a phone call from Hamisi. "Yes. You mean he called? What did he say?"

"Well, I asked him if he wanted to leave a phone number, but he wouldn't. He left an e-mail address, and he wanted you to e-mail him. Here it is," she said, as she handed Lloyd the piece of paper where she had written it down.

"Hamisi is very secretive and protective of his identity," Lloyd said as he looked at the e-mail address, which was a Hotmail account and could be created free of charge to use for temporary communication. "He won't give me his phone number, and I'm not sure if he even has a phone. I didn't see a landline when I went to his apartment. He's probably on cell phone communication only, and he might even use disposable ones that cannot be traced."

"I'm going to e-mail him right now," Lloyd continued. "If he reached out to me, it must be important."

"Aren't you going to eat first, Lloyd? You've had a long day."

"I'll e-mail him first. Then I'll eat, and by the time I finish, maybe he will have responded."

"Well, if you want to use your laptop at your desk, I'll bring a plate to you with your tray so you can eat while you work," said Stephanie, as she headed toward the kitchen.

"That would be great, honey," Lloyd said, as he headed to his home office. He logged onto his laptop and accessed his Microsoft Outlook account. Hamisi provided an e-mail address of **pusela@hotmail.com**. Lloyd remembered Hamisi mentioning Pusela as the body of water his ancestors navigated during their ancient travels.

Lloyd sent Hamisi the following message: *My wife told me you wanted to reach me. Would you like me to visit you tomorrow?*

He thought it best to keep it short and sweet, since he wasn't sure why Hamisi had called. Stephanie walked into Lloyd's office carrying the tray which held his dinner.

"Here's your dinner, honey," said Stephanie. "Are you going to be in here a while?"

"Yes. I'm going to surf the Net while I'm waiting for Hamisi to respond to my e-mail message. Are you going to be up much longer?"

"I'm going to read for a little while and then go to bed. You know I have to get up early tomorrow for a meeting with teachers in my department before school starts. Don't be too late," she said, winking at the same time.

"I won't. Once I hear from Hamisi, I'll be right up to bed," said Lloyd, as he looked at Stephanie and winked back at her, anticipating the night of ecstasy to come.

After Stephanie left the room, Lloyd began surfing news sites on the Web. Nearly every major news organization had the story about the Houston kidnapping on its web site's home pages. Some of the stories even included Lloyd's photo. As a local reporter, he had worked in obscurity for so long, this new found notoriety was a bit unsettling, but nice.

Then a message notice popped up on the screen, indicating that Lloyd had received an e-mail. It was from Hamisi.

I'd like to see you. Meet me tomorrow morning at 10 o'clock where the fountains are at the Lake on Post Oak complex. Are you familiar with the location?

Lloyd responded: *Yes. It's not far from where you live. Where will you be?*

Hamisi's reply, which arrived within a couple of minutes, said: *I'll be sitting on one of the benches in front of the lake. Please come alone.*

I'll be there, replied Lloyd, as he pushed the send button. Hamisi's constant cloak-and-dagger routine was both frustrating and intriguing. Lloyd closed his laptop, turned off the light in his office, and headed upstairs, all the while wondering why Hamisi had such a sense of urgency about meeting him.

CHAPTER 23

When Lloyd and Charles left Ed Jackson's office on the day the Pauley baby was found, the editor pounded his fist on the top of his walnut desk. His face reddened as he thought about what had just happened. How dare Lloyd be so heavy-handed with him! Ed couldn't believe the change in Lloyd which seemingly occurred overnight.

Before this latest episode, Lloyd had been a docile, compliant reporter who had little ambition and did not make waves. He did what he was told without any back talk. The Pauley incident and the way it had transpired had turned Lloyd into a troublemaker—Ed was sure of it. Lloyd had the audacity to make demands, as if Ed was the underling and Lloyd was the boss.

Ed had known there was going to be trouble when the boys upstairs forced him to meet their predetermined racial quota in the reporting pool. Those guys could sit back, smoke cigars in the expensive lounge chairs at the country club and pat themselves on the back about what a fantastic job they were doing with diversity among the staff.

Meanwhile, Ed was in the trenches, trying to keep readers interested enough to buy newspapers while simultaneously juggling the demands of a workplace that was a multicultural cauldron, always on the brink of exploding. There were constant arguments, rivalries and emotional flair-ups.

Ten years ago, the powers that be had forced Ed to hire at least one additional black reporter as window dressing. After all, the paper had to be politically correct in a metro area with half a million black residents. Now he had an out-of-control nigger on his hands and he was going to have to do something about it.

It wasn't as though he had anything against blacks as a race. He just thought some of them didn't know their place. Affirmative action couldn't make up for what an employee lacked in fundamentals, and it was common knowledge that blacks simply couldn't compete with whites when it came to English and grammar skills, nor did they have the same intellectual aptitude. Look at how low they scored on SAT tests, for Christ's sake! And why were they always late for appointments?

Lloyd's reporting was proficient. If Ed sent him on an assignment, he could obtain the basic five w's of who, what, when, where and why.

Every newspaper needed those types of reporters. But if Lloyd continued to believe he could call the shots, there was no telling how far he'd take it.

To further complicate things, the *Ledger* was receiving accolades from media outlets around the country for the way the paper had handled the entire Pauley kidnapping escapade. The paper was being hailed worldwide as an operation that had its finger on the pulse of the local community.

The executives at the paper had, in fact, called Ed into the corporate suites to congratulate him. They actually presented him with a bonus check and gave him a raise. But the success came with a high price tag, and Ed had not mastered the fine art of hiding his true feelings behind his facial expressions. He was, in two words, pissed off.

Ed had been in the newspaper business his entire life. As an adolescent in the early 1960s, he had earned spending money by delivering the *Houston Ledger* in his working-class Heights neighborhood. He vividly remembered riding his bicycle in the summer heat and autumn rain, tossing papers early mornings before school started.

While he was in college majoring in journalism, Ed was editor of the University of Houston campus newspaper, *The Daily Cougar*, and during his senior year completed an internship at the *Ledger*.

After graduation, he was hired as a researcher for the Metro section of the paper. When he started in the business, stories were typed on IBM Selectric typewriters with no memory or correction capabilities, let alone spell check features.

Over the next twenty years, he had scratched and clawed his way up the corporate ladder, competing against others in the paper who had what he didn't have — a wealthy pedigree or family connections in the newspaper business. He had finally become editor in 1989.

He'd spent more than twenty years guiding the paper through its heyday in the 1990s and keeping it afloat as news gradually — then rapidly — moved from newsprint to the Internet. In all of his years as editor he had never been bullied by one of his reporters, and he'd be damned if he was going to let Lloyd Palmer force him into a corner.

There had to be a way to bring Lloyd's ego back down to earth, and Ed was determined to find a way to do it. Bob Murray, one of his old buddies from the neighborhood, would know how to handle Lloyd. Ed hadn't spoken with Bob, whom everyone called "Bubba," in several years, but they had known each other since grammar school.

Bob used to be the bully in the school yard, terrorizing the kids who were small in stature or who were too afraid to defend themselves. He amassed a pocket full of change every week by taking the lunch money off a lot of the kids in the younger grades. Fortunately for Ed, his older brother was just as tough as Bob was, so he was never a victim of Bob's antics.

The tough-guy attitude didn't wear off once Bob became an adult. He still participated in the occasional barroom brawl. And the two of them didn't operate in the same social circles, but Ed had contacted him before in situations where gentle persuasion wasn't enough. Ed picked up the phone and dialed his number. Bob didn't answer, so Ed left a voice mail message.

"Bob, this is Ed. I need to talk with you about something. Meet me tomorrow evening at six at the Fuddruckers near Greenway Plaza. It's important."

CHAPTER 24

Lloyd arrived at the Lake on Post Oak complex at quarter to ten the next morning. He wanted to be certain to be positioned when Hamisi arrived. The complex was a well-maintained piece of property in Houston's Galleria area, containing three glass office buildings that were several stories high. In the center of the complex was a man-made lake with a fountain.

White ducks and geese paddled across the lake, and there were several park benches positioned around it. It was a perfect spot for a picnic or a romantic rendezvous. Lloyd also noticed that it was an ideal place to meet someone because, if anyone approached, they could be viewed from any number of angles.

Lloyd drove into the covered parking facility, parked his car and walked over to one of the park benches. He didn't see anyone sitting on any of the benches, so he picked one of them, sat down and waited.

Lloyd had called the office to let Ed know he would be coming in around noon. He had been putting in a lot of hours while working on the Pauley kidnapping story, so Ed didn't seem to mind.

But the *Ledger* was still receiving calls from other news outlets, and Lloyd needed to be on hand to respond to inquiries and assist other staff members with continued updates. He checked his watch and hoped that Hamisi would show up soon.

"I'm glad you're on time," said Hamisi from behind him, startling Lloyd. "You have had a very busy week, my friend."

"Hamisi, where did you come from? I almost jumped off this bench when you spoke. How did you get here without me seeing you?"

"I arrived early and staked out a position where I could see everything. I wanted to meet here for that reason."

"You're right. It has been a busy week. My whole world has been turned upside down."

Hamisi's expression became serious. "Now do you understand why everything that is written down is not truth? Your newspaper had the whole city in chaos because of a completely false report about a kidnapping."

"No need to rub it in. I've been living under the illusion that the goal of my profession was to present the truth and the facts. I know now that there's a lot more to it than that and that what we print can leave so many lives hanging in the balance. Meeting you has changed my life, Hamisi."

"My universe has been altered as well, my friend," Hamisi replied, and then he paused reflectively. "I wanted to talk with you before I left town."

"Leaving town? Why are you being so secretive? Did something happen?"

"Yes, something happened. The speed of your journey along the road to true knowledge has increased in the past several days. This means that some of your co-workers may eventually become aware of me, and it is important that I remain an unknown quantity. As a griot, I must remain outside the limelight. My mind must remain unencumbered by the distractions of this world. A griot must deny self for the greater good. There can be no desire for fortune or fame."

Lloyd's heart sank. "Hamisi, you can't disappear on me now. I'm just beginning to understand some of the things you've been talking about. This whole Pauley fiasco has opened my eyes to the fallacy of what I and other reporters do every day at the *Ledger*."

"You give me too much credit, my son," replied Hamisi. "I believe you would have made these discoveries on your own . . . eventually."

"But I was planning to do more research and write an extensive article about you and the Lemba tribe. Maybe get it into the *Ledger* or some other large circulation publication. I think I have my editor's attention now, and he's more open to listen to my ideas."

"You can still do your research, Lloyd, but I cannot be part of your story. As I told you, griots must be inconspicuous, nearly anonymous to the public."

"Why, Hamisi? Your wisdom could help so many, could open so many eyes."

"Because, my son, if a griot becomes a—what's the word in American culture—ah, a 'celebrity,' then his oral record will be subject to manipulation by others. His record will no longer be pure and will thus become unreliable. Our people depend upon us to pass our history from generation to generation."

"Lloyd, continue with your research. There are many ways besides contact with me that you can develop your story. There is a group called the Lemba Cultural Association that can give you much of the data you seek. You should be able to make contact with them online."

"What is more important, Lloyd, is that you learn more about yourself and what could be the origins of your ancestors. Do you have a Bible at home?"

Lloyd thought about the Bible that Stephanie had given him a few years ago for Father's Day. He knew it was at the house somewhere but had no idea where he'd put it. "More than one," he said, "although I'm ashamed to admit that I rarely crack it open. Why is that important?"

"Read Genesis, chapter 2 verse 13, and chapter 10. You will learn much about the origins of man and the descendants of Noah's son, Ham. After the Great Flood, it was the descendants of Ham who populated all of the black races of the Earth."

"I'm not very religious, Hamisi. Most of the time when I've read the Bible or when I hear verses quoted, they're in this antiquated language with a lot of 'thee's' and 'thou's.' I can't make head or tail of what's in there."

"That's because you have to read it with an open mind, an open heart. If your mind is closed, neither knowledge nor wisdom can enter."

"Okay, Hamisi, if you say so. I'll do it. When are you coming back to Houston?"

"I'm not sure when or if I will be back. My work here may be done, and I can move on to another location. But if you need to reach me, you have my e-mail address."

"Will I ever see you again?"

"Are we now indeed friends, Lloyd?"

"Hamisi, I believe you are one of the most important friends I will ever meet."

"Then, as friends, we will always be connected, seeing each other perhaps not with our physical eyes, but by using our other senses, including our sixth sense — our spiritual sense."

"I'll never forget you, Hamisi," Lloyd said, as he shook his friend's hand and then embraced him.

"Nor will I you," Hamisi replied, then he turned and walked away.

CHAPTER 25

"I'll kill you," is what the attacker, Rodney Dennis, said, according to neighborhood eyewitnesses whom Lloyd interviewed when Ed assigned him to a stabbing incident in a Northwest Houston subdivision. After Lloyd met with Hamisi, Ed had called and sent him to the neighborhood because the story might have regional implications.

Houston had acquired thousands of new residents from New Orleans in 2005 in the aftermath of Hurricane Katrina. Some of the natives of the Big Easy were still living hand-to-mouth, with multiple families living in homes that were designed as single-family dwellings.

Such was the case with this latest crime victim. Lloyd had spoken to Brenda Dickerson, one of the women who lived in the home with Rodney. Brenda had lived in Houston since that unfortunate August a few years ago when the New Orleans levees burst. She and her sisters, Regina and Latoya, were separated by the storm's upheaval and reunited a month later.

Regina was Rodney's girlfriend and neither had been able to find steady work since arriving in Houston. They and their two boys sometimes had to resort to staying in homeless shelters just to avoid sleeping on the streets.

Latoya's live-in lover, Curtis, who she called her "boo," was the stabbing victim. The three sisters, their boyfriends, and their combined six children were all sharing a three-bedroom home in Houston's FM 1960 area.

"Mama always expected me to look out for Regina and Latoya, since I'm the oldest," Brenda told Lloyd, "but they were always cussin' and fussin' and arguing. Something bad was bound to happen sooner or later."

"By 'they,' I assume you mean Rodney and Curtis?" asked Lloyd.

"Yeah, them two didn't like each other, and they were always trying to prove who was the toughest, who had the most heart. They reminded me of those deer with the horns that you see on the *National Geographic* channel, buckin' and pushin' up against each other to see who'll take over the territory.

"I guess one of 'em had to prove who was boss. The thing is that I rented this house for all of us, so neither one of them was really in charge anyway. Is Curtis going to make it?"

"The ambulance took him to the hospital. He lost a lot of blood," said Lloyd, as he nodded toward the blood-stained area across the street, not far from where they stood, that had been roped off by the sheriff with yellow crime scene tape. The argument between the two men had begun inside but had escalated steadily and moved outside.

According to Brenda and the neighbors, Rodney yelled, "I'll kill you," and stabbed Curtis in the abdomen and chest several times. Apparently, the argument was over forty dollars that Rodney thought Curtis stole from the box his son had hidden under his bed.

"I sure hope he makes it," said Brenda, "because, if he doesn't, neither of my sisters will have their men with them. Rodney will go to jail, and Curtis will be gone forever. Our family has been through enough grief. I don't know how much more we can take," she said, and she began sobbing.

Brenda then peered at Lloyd curiously. "Aren't you that reporter who was on T.V. last night about that River Oaks lady and the kidnapping?"

"Yes m'am, I am."

"Well, you sure did a good deed. Too bad more reporters don't help our city like you did. Most of 'em just want to take advantage of people when they're already down and out."

"It's mostly done out of habit and training, m'am. It's not personal," said Lloyd, but as soon as he uttered the words, he wished he could retract them. He realized how callous and insensitive he sounded.

"Well, if they are in everybody's personal business, that sure makes it personal," replied Brenda with an air of indignation.

"I'm sorry, I misspoke," said Lloyd. "What I meant was that they really don't mean any harm. They've been taught by their bosses and others in their profession to obtain the juiciest possible details for their stories in order to sell newspapers. Sometimes they forget there are real people's lives involved."

"You're damned right," said Brenda, as she put her hands on her hips and cocked her head to the right. "Your reporter friends need to get their act together."

Lloyd's cell phone rang. "Excuse me one second," he told Brenda as he hit the send button and walked a few feet away so he could have some privacy.

"Lloyd, are you still at the scene of that stabbing in Northwest Houston?" asked Ed.

"Yes, Ed. Is there something you need me to do?"

"It's now a murder case. The victim died on the way to the hospital."

"All right, Ed. I'm here with one of the women who lived in the same house with him. Is it okay to break the news to her?"

"Why not? She'll find out soon enough anyway. When you do the write up on this one, you probably should work in some info about the continued plight of the New Orleans transplants since Katrina."

"I'd already thought of that, Ed, and I'm on it."

"When you're done there, you need to come back here as soon as possible. We're still getting interview requests from some of the other dailies and news networks, and we want the visual backdrop to be the *Ledger* newsroom."

"That'll work. I've been receiving text messages all day from newspapers and magazines from all over. *Time* magazine may want me to do an exclusive. They're even talking about a cover story."

"All interviews have to first be cleared through my office."

"Ed, I understand protocol, but if *Time* magazine wants me for a cover story, I'm taking it—period. It's too big an opportunity for me to walk away from it."

Ed's suspicions were correct. Last week, Lloyd would have responded with a simple, "Yes, Ed." But Lloyd's attitude had definitely changed and there was no way to put the genie back in the bottle.

"Just get back here as soon as possible. We want to make sure we get the interviews done for the outlets' afternoon deadlines."

"As soon as I inform Ms. Dickerson about Curtis' death, I'll head that way," replied Lloyd, but he heard the phone disconnect halfway through his sentence. Ed had hung up.

Lloyd hit cancel to end the call and walked in Brenda's direction. "Brenda, I'm sorry, but I have some bad news."

Brenda took two apprehensive steps backward. "What is it? Who was that on the phone?"

"It was my editor. One of our sources at the hospital called and said that Curtis died in the ambulance on the way there. He's gone. I'm sorry."

"Oh my Lord," Brenda wailed. "'Toya's gonna be heartbroken."

CHAPTER 26

Ed arrived at Fuddrucker's a few minutes early and found a booth that was surrounded by the fewest customers. He and Bubba shared an appetite for great hamburgers — thick, juicy and medium rare. None of those fast food, frozen patty burgers for them. They had eaten at Fuddrucker's many times, and when they wanted to get loose with a couple of chicks after work, this is where they brought them.

Ed sat in the booth facing the door so he could see Bubba when he arrived. Bubba walked in at 6:00 p.m. sharp, wearing his signature cowboy hat, boots and jeans. With his full gray beard, six-foot-four-inch frame and a girth carrying about 250 pounds, Bubba was an imposing figure.

Ed waved to get Bubba's attention and directed him over to the booth. "Hi, Bubba. You're looking good. Helen must be treating you right," he said, referring to Bubba's wife.

"Helen and about five other chicks, but what else is new? Did you order yet?"

"No, I was waiting for you to get here. I got the menus though."

A waitress stopped at the table to take their orders. When she was gone, Bubba turned his attention to Ed.

"So, Ed, what do you need from me?"

"How do you know I need something? I could have just wanted us to get together to talk about old times."

"Who are you kidding? The only time you call me is when you want me to do your dirty work. Since you left the old neighborhood and went to college, you've barely set foot in our old stomping grounds. And you can't get your hands too dirty since you hob-nob with the fat cats downtown and with the high society folks," Bubba said sarcastically.

"Well, if you must know, I do have a problem at work. There's a boy—a nigger—who's getting out of hand. It's not entirely uncontrollable yet, but it's moving in that direction. I wanted to have a game plan ready just in case I need it."

"I told you that would happen once they started getting their bylines in the paper. Those coons think they practically own the *Ledger* now, don't they?"

"It's not everybody, just this particular one. You know the guy who broke the story on the Pauley kidnapping?"

"Yeah, I heard about it. I can't believe the city handed out welfare checks to those idiots. Most of them probably deserved to be in jail anyway. I'll bet some other reporter did the work and that coon wants to take the credit. That's just like a nigger."

"This time, Bubba, he actually did break the story. It's gone straight to his head, and he's practically giving me orders. I can't fire him because now he's not only a hero to the newspaper but a hero to this city. *Time* magazine called him for a cover story, for Christ's sake. Something may need to be done soon."

"What do you want me to do?"

"Nothing yet, but just be on standby and think of some way to scare the bejesus out of him. I'll let you know when."

"This time I'll need ten grand in cash."

"You'll get your money. Just be ready."

"You got it," Bubba replied, as the waitress delivered their hamburgers and they both enjoyed their meals.

CHAPTER 27

Lloyd got home shortly after 7:00 p.m., weary as a result of his long day. He had done back-to-back interviews from coast to coast with television, radio, print and electronic media. Clearly, Lloyd was experiencing his fifteen minutes of fame, as the name "Lloyd Palmer" was generating a palpable buzz on all the airwaves. Pretty soon, he'd probably need an agent, a publicist and an assistant, and the paparazzi would be gathering on his front lawn.

When he opened the door and walked into the foyer, he saw Stephanie in the den grading papers, something she did most evenings after dinner.

"Hi, Hon," she said. "You're late getting home again. I saw your interview on FOX News and you looked great."

"Yeah, the Pauley kidnapping story definitely has legs. It was an interesting enough topic to be included in another news cycle. But I'm beat. After I eat, I'd like to take a hot shower and go to bed."

"I saved a dinner plate for you in the kitchen. I can heat it up for you, if you like."

"No, go ahead and finish grading your papers. I'll do it myself."

Lloyd went to the kitchen and put his plate in the microwave. While his food was heating up, he remembered Hamisi's instructions for him to read the passages from Genesis. He had written down the scripture references on his notepad, and he pulled it out of the left breast pocket of his shirt.

"Stephanie, where do we keep our Bibles?" he yelled from the kitchen.

"In here, on the bookshelf. Why in the world are you asking me about the Bibles? I'm trying to remember the last time I saw you reading one, and I can't."

"There's something that Hamisi wanted me to look up in the book of Genesis."

"Wow, after knowing Hamisi for only a few weeks, he has gotten you to do something I've been trying to get you to do for years," replied Stephanie, as she laughed. "I'm impressed."

"Ha, ha, very funny. I'll look it up after I eat."

After dinner, Lloyd went to the den, found the Bible on the second shelf and carried it with him to his office. "I'll be in here a while," he told Stephanie, "so if you need something let me know."

"It's going to take me another hour to finish grading these papers, then I'm going to bed. Don't stay up too late, hon."

"I won't. I just want to get this done while it's on my mind."

Lloyd sat down at his desk and opened the Bible to its first book. He was familiar with some of the commonly repeated phrases about the creation story such as "in the beginning" and "let there be light," but had never sat down and read Bible passages himself. For most of his life, he had thought that the Bible was just an ancient book of religious tales, nothing more.

Stephanie had tried to get him to attend weekly Bible study services with her, with little success. When he did attend, it was mostly out of obligation, in an effort to keep her reasonably happy about his participation. Even when he was in Sunday services, his mind often drifted elsewhere. All of the death and destruction he had seen during his twenty years as a reporter had led him to question God's purpose.

But meeting Hamisi had made him more aware — and more curious — about the link between the primeval past and the contemporary present. Hamisi said the Lemba's oral records went back at least one hundred generations, which would put the date at about two thousand years ago, shortly after the birth of Christ.

He turned to the second chapter of Genesis and began reading at verse ten. *"A river went out of Eden to water the garden; and from thence it was parted, and became into four heads."* He then read the thirteenth verse, as Hamisi had instructed. *"And the name of the second river is Gihon: the same is it that compasseth the whole land of Ethiopia."*

The verse identified the location of the garden of Eden at least partially within the nation of Ethiopia, on the African continent. "Can this be true?" Lloyd said aloud, to no one but himself. If so, he thought, why had he not heard about it before?

Lloyd decided to go online to do some research about Ethiopia. He found a map of the world during Biblical times, and the location of Ethiopia was roughly the same then as it is now. Apparently, the Biblical account had been validated by science, Lloyd found, since Ethiopia is also one of the oldest sites of human existence known to archaeologists.

As Lloyd continued to surf the Internet, he came across a reference to Flora Shaw Lugard, also known as "Lady Lugard," who wrote *A Tropical Dependency*, the first general survey of African people in world history. Lady Lugard described the ancient Ethiopians as "the tallest, most beautiful and long-lived of the human races."

Lloyd viewed image after image of peoples who were native to the east African country. The indigenous people to the area had, and still have, very dark skin. For all Lloyd knew, the ancient Ethiopians may have been his ancestors' cousins, a possibility which both fascinated and empowered him.

For the first time, Lloyd felt connected to the very origins of man. He felt powerful, as though nothing, no force on earth, could stand in his way ever again. Yes, he was a husband, a father, a reporter; but that night he became much more. He became a man on a mission—the exact nature of which he was sure would become clear to him soon. His friend Hamisi would help him find his way to it.

CHAPTER 28

The next day at work went smoothly for Lloyd. He was still receiving interview requests, but the intensity had waned a bit. Ed hadn't given him a news assignment since he'd arrived at 9:00 a.m., but Lloyd figured Ed wanted to keep him available to speak to the media.

Audrey, the office vixen, had volunteered to help field some of the calls, but Lloyd didn't want her directly involved with his business. Knowing her, she'd spread rumors that the two of them got together after work to discuss story ideas, and that he confided in her about his sources. Besides, Charles could take care of any calls that Lloyd couldn't handle.

Time magazine had called to confirm the cover story, and a photographer was coming to the *Ledger* tomorrow to take his picture. It was amazing what a difference a few days could make.

Two weeks ago, he was feeling sorry for himself, thinking that his career had dead-ended. Now he felt like the sky was the limit and that his reporting could actually make a difference.

He had selected journalism as a career to become a good newsman and potentially a hero to his community. He wanted to cast himself in the mold of Bob Woodward and Carl Bernstein — the two *Washington Post* reporters who had broken the Watergate case and unraveled Richard Nixon's presidency. Mostly, he wanted to make his parents proud; they'd sacrificed everything so he could get his college education.

He had some free time, so he decided to Google the Lemba tribe again to see what he could find. He sifted through the listings he had not accessed previously to see which ones were relevant. It wasn't that the Lembas were a secret society because there were dozens of maps, research papers and photographs of Lemba tribesmen online. But knowledge of their existence seemed to be limited to the arenas of genetic science and anthropology. It was as though they were hidden in plain sight. Lloyd's story would bring them out of the shadows of obscurity.

Lloyd checked the notes he had made previously and came across the name of the professor who was giving a lecture at Rice University in a few days. He felt that now would be a good time to make contact.

Dr. Gastalt was a professor at the University of Chicago's School of Genetic Science and had written a thesis on some of the less populous African tribes, including the Lemba. Gastalt had actually lived among the Lemba people for a few months ten years ago. Meeting with the professor could uncover more details.

Lloyd found Gastalt's office phone number and decided to call him. He hoped the professor kept regular office hours. The phone rang twice, and the professor answered.

"Hello, Gastalt here."

"Dr. Gastalt, my name is Lloyd Palmer, and I'm a reporter for the *Houston Ledger*. How are you?"

"I'm fine, Mr. Palmer. How can I help you?" The professor sounded impatient.

"I understand you'll be at Rice University next week, and I'm writing an extensive article about the Lemba tribe. I was wondering if I could meet with you while you're in town to add to my research and get some insights from you."

"Well, well, well," Gastalt replied, as his tone changed from one of impatience to one of intrigue. "That's interesting. I rarely receive inquiries about the Lemba. People either don't know or don't care to know about them. They're an enigmatic group to the majority of the Earth's population."

"I am quite interested, sir, and have actually met a member of the tribe here in town," said Lloyd, relieved that the professor was willing to talk.

"I find that hard to believe. The Lemba rarely leave the African continent and, when they do, they seldom reveal their identity."

Lloyd pressed forward. "I did meet one of the Lemba griots, in the flesh, and I think this story would be of interest to our readers. So may I meet you during your stay here in Houston?"

"I'll only be there for a couple of days, but I think I can fit you into my schedule. How much of my time will you need?"

"An hour or two should do it."

"I'll give you my cell phone number, which is (773) 555-4793. I arrive on Tuesday and will be there until Thursday evening. Let's plan to meet on Wednesday for dinner."

Lloyd entered the phone number into his cell phone. "Thank you very much, Professor Gastalt. I look forward to meeting you. Goodbye."

Lloyd hung up the phone and was encouraged by the way everything seemed to be coming together. The background information he received from Hamisi, his Internet research, and his interview with Gastalt would be more than enough to form the foundation of his article. An on-the-record interview with an actual member of the Lembas would bring the tribe to life for the readers, whether the article appeared in the *Ledger* or elsewhere.

His desk phone rang and he answered. "Lloyd Palmer here."

"I hate to pull you away from your celebrity activities," said Ed, his words laced with sarcasm, "but I have an assignment for you. Come to my office and I'll brief you on the details."

"I'll be right there, Ed."

Lloyd had decided that he'd be cooperative with Ed until he weighed his options. No need to rock the boat now when his star power had risen in the industry. Potential employers would be watching to see how he handled his new-found fame.

If he displayed signs of having an out-of-control ego or being difficult to work with, it could go against him. He had to bide his time until he determined his next move.

Lloyd went to Ed's office and sat in the chair facing the editor's desk. "What's up, Ed?"

"This one is really ugly, Lloyd. Some crimes are almost unimaginable, but the crazier the crime, the more details our readers demand and the more papers we sell."

Lloyd had worked with Ed long enough to know that if he was exhibiting any signs of having a conscience, then something horrendous must have happened. "What is it, Ed?"

"A young woman was killed by her boyfriend, who cut up her body and then barbecued the parts on a grill. He then put the remains in garbage bags and dumped the bags in a landfill. The police took him in for questioning and are trying to get a confession out of him."

Lloyd was stunned. "You've got to be kidding. Was he high on drugs or just plain crazy?"

"Apparently, he was of a sound enough mind to calculate a way to avoid detection. He seems to be fairly normal mentally, according to the police."

Lloyd still couldn't believe what he was hearing. "Who was the victim?"

"You remember, Keisha Smith, the freshman at Texas Southern University who's been missing for the past week?"

"Yeah. I saw her mother on the news asking the authorities to help find her daughter. She seemed pretty shaken up."

"Well, evidently, the young lady was living with this guy who was much older than she was, and the guy had a nasty jealous streak. The cops aren't sure exactly what happened, but they think he went into a jealous rage and killed her with his bare hands.

"Cutting up the body was his way of hiding the evidence; but then he figured the body could be identified through DNA, and the cops would put two and two together. So he put the parts on the grill to destroy the evidence."

"That's just plain gruesome," responded Lloyd, with a look of incredulity. "There are some sick people in this world."

"The funny thing is . . . well, I guess it's not so funny, but 'macabre' would be a better word. Anyway, some of the neighbors smelled the barbecuing, and it didn't smell like the usual steaks, ribs or hot dogs.

"They called the fire department to report the fumes because they thought the foul odor could be toxic or life threatening. The fire trucks came but, by then, the killer had doused the flames, and the firefighters couldn't find the source of the fumes."

"It sounds like they already have a lot of facts, Ed. They've caught the guy who did it. What would you like me to do?"

"Go to the county jail and see if you can get an interview with the suspect."

"Ed, that's not likely to happen. His attorney won't let me anywhere near him. Anything that the suspect tells me, and is subsequently reported in the paper, could be used against him in court."

"Maybe you could use your new-found celebrity status to gain access to him," Ed said, only half jokingly.

"I think it's a complete waste of time, Ed. But if you insist, I'll go."

"Yes, I insist. You can't spend all day here waiting around for Oprah or *Rolling Stone* magazine to call you. Besides, you might get lucky."

"I'm not sitting around waiting for phone calls, Ed. The calls are coming in with no effort or interference from me. It's good for the paper to get this type of positive exposure. I would think you'd be happy about it."

"It does help the paper. I just don't want you to forget that your job here is as a reporter, not head of the PR department," Ed responded with contempt.

"I'm well aware of my job title and description, Ed. But in light of what's happened, I may be weighing other options."

"Is that some sort of threat, Lloyd?"

"No, sir. Not a threat, more of a recommendation that you acknowledge that things may have changed at the *Ledger* as far as I and my position are concerned."

Ed's face reddened with smoldering anger. "As long as you work for me as a reporter in my department, that's a linear relationship that always has me on top and you on the bottom. Is that clear enough for you?"

"As a bell, sir," Lloyd responded as he sat upright in his chair, knowing he had gotten under Ed's skin but trying to contain the smirk he wanted to let loose on his face.

"Now, go to the county jail and try to get an interview with the murderer. His name is Earl Allen Griffin."

"Okay, Ed. As you said, I might get lucky."

CHAPTER 29

When Lloyd arrived at the Harris County Jail he parked his car, turned off the ignition and sat in it for awhile. There was no way that Griffin's attorney would let him conduct an interview for publication. It was likely that Griffin would either plea bargain to avoid the death penalty or would enter a plea of not guilty by reason of insanity if the case were to go to trial. Any admission of guilt in a news article would clearly not be in Griffin's best interest. Lloyd had to come up with a strategy to convince the attorney that telling Griffin's side of the story would be helpful — even financially beneficial.

Lloyd had mixed feelings about even being there. He considered Griffin to be a monster, a self-centered sociopath who, after killing his lover in a fit of rage, committed an act denying the victim's family the comfort of closure after the death of their loved one. Cutting up Keisha Smith's body and burning the parts elicited the worst kind of human depravity, and conjured up images and pain that no mother should have to endure. Since the details of the murder had been released, Keisha's mother had been prescribed a mild sedative, was on bed rest, and was under a doctor's care.

Lloyd was conflicted: On the one hand he didn't think a sociopath like Griffin deserved to be elevated in the media. On the other hand, as a journalist, he knew that obtaining an interview of this caliber was the stuff about which reporters had wet dreams. There was no downside, professionally, to conducting a one-on-one with Griffin. None whatsoever.

Then Lloyd had an idea. If he could guarantee Griffin's attorney that the contents of the interview would not be published until after the verdict had been rendered, then he might get Griffin's approval. Lloyd doubted that Griffin would be found not guilty; the evidence against him was too damning. But the constitutional protections against double jeopardy meant that Griffin could not be tried twice for the same crime. So an admission of guilt after the verdict would incur no legal consequences.

Lloyd planned to leave his cell phone and other valuables in the car, since visitors weren't allowed to bring items into the jail. He popped the trunk of his car so he could put his brief bag and cell phone inside. As he took his cell phone out of his pocket, he received a text message: *Remember that truth must be protected at all costs.* – Hamisi

Lloyd had become accustomed to Hamisi's words of wisdom, but they always seemed to be delivered at random times. Yet Lloyd had learned that Hamisi's witticisms were often prescient: within hours or days after making his statements, a situation occurred confirming the essence of Hamisi's words.

After putting everything in his trunk and with a credible plan in mind, Lloyd exited his car and walked toward the main building of the prison facility. There were a dozen or so people in line, most of them black, waiting to go through the metal detectors so they could visit loved ones who were incarcerated.

"Please write down the name of the prisoner you are here to see on this form," the guard told Lloyd when he got to the front counter.

"I'm here to see Earl Allen Griffin, sir."

"The gas grill killer? His attorney is with him now, so you'll have to wait. Are you a family member?"

"No, sir. I'm a reporter for the *Ledger*."

"Normally attorneys don't allow their clients to talk to reporters. You'll have to wait until he comes out and get his permission."

The guard did a double take. "Wait a minute. Aren't you that reporter who solved the River Oaks kidnapping?"

"You got 'em, that's me, Lloyd Palmer. How long do you think the attorney will be?"

The guard completely ignored his question, instead announcing Lloyd's presence to the other guards. "Hey, y'all. This is Lloyd Palmer, the reporter who found out that lady killed her own baby."

The guards all gave Lloyd a round of applause, as the one he had been talking to turned toward him. "Man, thanks for getting the police off our backs. They were locking up brothers left and right." The guard shook Lloyd's hand vigorously.

"You're welcome. It's part of my job," responded Lloyd, something he was really starting to believe himself. The impact of him following his hunch was starting to sink in.

"My name is Melvin, sir. Melvin Banks. If there's anything I can do for you, Mr. Palmer, just say the word."

"Actually, there is something you can do. Do you have any idea how much longer it will be before Griffin's attorney comes out?"

"Let me check and see his arrival time," said Melvin, as he scanned the sign-in log.

"He got here at two o'clock, about an hour ago. He shouldn't be that much longer. You can wait here until he comes out. Can I get you anything to drink?"

"No, thank you. I'm fine. I'll just wait here. It's important that I speak with him today," Lloyd said as he sat down on the bench in the waiting area. "Can you tell me the attorney's name?"

Melvin surveyed the sign-in sheet again. "His name is David Rosenfeld, sir."

"Okay, thanks."

Lloyd hadn't been to a lot of jails when covering stories because he focused primarily on the crime scenes, the victims and their families. But now he'd been to jails twice within a few days—once to get his friend Ron out and now to try to get this interview. He'd have to be very convincing to persuade Rosenfeld to allow Griffin to talk.

While Lloyd waited, he sat and watched the people coming and going through the visitation line. They were mostly women, presumably girlfriends or wives of the inmates; some had children with them. From the way they were dressed, most were relatively poor.

The way the criminal justice system worked, the side on which the scales of justice tilted was directly related to one's ability to obtain adequate legal representation. Those on the lower rungs of the economic ladder didn't have the means to get competent lawyers. Most depended on court appointed attorneys who were too busy or incompetent to adequately represent their clients.

Lloyd knew that a few wrong choices in high school might have landed him behind bars rather than on the path to college and a career. He shook his head and buried his face in his hands as he thought about what could have been.

Lloyd felt a hand on his shoulder. It was Melvin.

"Mr. Palmer, Mr. Rosenfeld is coming out now," Melvin said, as he nodded toward a man with a navy blue pinstriped suit and red silk necktie.

Lloyd stood and approached him. "Mr. Rosenfeld, I'm Lloyd Palmer with the *Ledger*. Can I speak with you for a moment?"

"If it's about interviewing my client, then you're wasting your time," he said, as he signed the log indicating his departure time.

"Please, Mr. Rosenfeld. Just hear me out."

The attorney frowned. "Okay, Mr. Palmer. Let's sit over here," pointing in the direction of a bench that was furthest away from the gathering crowd of visitors.

As they sat down, Rosenfeld said, "By the way, Mr. Palmer, good work on the kidnapping case. You really kept the city from getting a black eye on that one, pun intended."

Lloyd was beginning to like the attention he was getting. "You really should thank my mother. I was planning on leaving it alone and doing routine reporting. She convinced me to follow my hunch."

"You can thank her from all of us in the city, really. Now how can I help you?"

"I'd like to interview Mr. Griffin," Lloyd said and held up his hand. "Now before you say no, hear me out. I know that a news report before the trial could be incriminating for your client and might even be against legal ethics."

"You're damned right it would be. I'm not going to risk getting sanctioned by the Bar Association. Maybe even disbarred."

"Mr. Rosenfeld, there wouldn't be any risk to you or your client. Here's what I'm proposing. Let me do an exclusive interview. Earl can tell his side of what happened. I'll record the interview, but I won't publish the story until after the trial is over."

"Mr. Palmer, I don't think you'd be able to sit on a story of this magnitude for that long. What if your editor forces you to run the story? Then my client will be screwed, along with my legal career.

"I've dealt with you reporters before," Rosenfeld added. "I don't trust any of you as far as I can throw you. Why not wait until after the trial to conduct the interview?"

"Call me Lloyd, please. Mr. Rosenfeld, I know you have a right to be skeptical, but I give you my solemn word that I won't even replay the recording until after the trial is over. I'd rather conduct the interview now while the details are fresh in Griffin's mind. Months from now, some of it will be forgotten."

"Okay, Lloyd. Let's say I believe you. But you do have a boss. What if your editor forces the issue?"

Lloyd pondered the question for a few seconds. He could feel Rosenfeld's resolve weakening. There had to be a way to close the deal once and for all. Hamisi had told him to protect the truth at all costs. Lloyd had been trained to view the truth as something that should be exposed, not protected. Sometimes he wished Hamisi wouldn't speak in riddles; it was all so confounding. Then he had an idea.

"Here's what we'll do. Once I tape the interview with Earl, I'll put the flash drive in a safe deposit box and leave it there until the trial is over. I will explain your terms to my editor and get him to understand the reasons behind it. He probably won't like it; but he won't have access to the key, and I'll keep the information between us.

"As a reporter, I have the constitutional right to protect my sources. I would go to jail for contempt of court before I would give up the location of the tape. Will you agree to do it now?"

Rosenfeld paused. He had taken Griffin's case pro bono, primarily to get the publicity so he could obtain future criminal clients. An exclusive spread in the *Ledger* after the trial ended would do him no harm and give him star power in his profession. He'd always wanted to join the ranks of America's famous defense lawyers, like Richard "Racehorse" Haynes, Mark Geragos and Johnnie Cochran. This could be his chance.

"Okay, Lloyd. I'm trusting that you'll keep your word. I've seen you handle yourself over the past few days, and I've been impressed by your integrity."

They shook hands. "Follow me, and I'll introduce you to Earl."

CHAPTER 30

Melvin pressed the button that buzzed Lloyd and Rosenfeld entry into the lockup facility. Lloyd had never been inside a jail before and started to get claustrophobic as he walked down the main corridor. There was an area inside where inmates could meet with their lawyers. A second guard ushered them into the meeting area.

"Sit here and wait," said the guard. "I'll bring Griffin to you in a few minutes."

While they waited, Lloyd thought it would be a good idea to get some background on Griffin from Rosenfeld in advance of the interview. "Do you think Griffin will cooperate?"

"Your guess is as good as mine," replied Rosenfeld. "He's no fool. He's fairly well educated, so he'll know that any statements he makes can be used by the prosecution to bolster their case. You'll need to convince him that the interview could be in his best interest."

"Fair enough," Lloyd responded.

The door then opened, and the guard escorted Griffin into the room. He was of average height and wore the orange jumpsuit worn by all of the inmates. His ankles were shackled, and his wrists were handcuffed.

"Mr. Rosenfeld, I thought you were gone," said Griffin, who then noticed Lloyd at the table. "Who's this?"

"This is Lloyd Palmer, a reporter for the *Houston Ledger.*"

"A reporter? Why in the hell would I want to talk to a reporter? Do you think I'm stupid?"

"Of course not, Earl. Lloyd has a proposition for you and I think you should hear him out."

"What's in it for me?"

"Just listen to what he has to say and then make your decision. Okay?"

Earl's placed his handcuffed hands on the table. He looked at Lloyd as if sizing him up. Earl thought his face looked familiar, but he couldn't figure out how he knew him. He doubted they had met face-to-face, but Earl knew he'd seen him somewhere before.

"What's up?" Griffin asked, nodding at Lloyd in recognition. "What are you selling?"

"What do you mean?" asked Lloyd.

"Everybody who wants to see me is selling something. You didn't come here because we're long lost friends, man, so what's up?"

"Do you know anything about the Pauley kidnapping?"

"Who doesn't? Some of the guys who were falsely arrested were in here on the cell block. They ought to bring that River Oaks broad in here with the rest of us brothers, and we'll show her what a bad guy really looks like. We'll make her feel right at home," he said as he smirked.

"This isn't about Mrs. Pauley, Earl. I asked you about it because I'm the reporter who broke the story."

"What? Are you thinking you can break this case wide open too? Man, the cops have already got the goods on me. Mr. Rosenfeld is working on a plea bargain so I won't get the needle."

"When it's all said and done, Earl, wouldn't you like to tell your side of the story?"

Earl was insistent. "Not until I get that plea bargain done."

"This is what I'd like to do, if you'll agree." Lloyd waited before proceeding so he would have Earl's full attention.

"I'd like to record your account of what happened between you and Keisha. I don't think you really meant to kill her. You just got angry and things got out of control, am I right?"

"I'm not going to admit anything just yet."

"Here's the deal, Earl. Once we finish the interview, the flash drive will be put in my safe deposit box. Mr. Rosenfeld will go with me to the bank and watch me put the flash drive in the box. I'll give him the key, so I won't have access to it on my own."

"What's to keep him from selling it to some other reporter? I don't trust lawyers or reporters. They're both scum, no more than a necessary evil. No offense."

"None taken. Rosenfeld won't be able to examine the contents of the box because it'll be in my name. I'll have to show my photo I.D., and they'll check my signature before they let me into the safety deposit box viewing area. But without the key, I won't be able to open the box. In other words, to retrieve the flash drive, both of us have to be present.

Lloyd continued. "There's something else you might want to consider."

"What's that?"

"Once the interview is published, there may be some interest from one of the major New York publishers offering you a book deal. You won't be able to benefit financially from your crime because of federal statute, but you could put the advance and royalties in a trust for a loved one, your mother perhaps."

Earl sat back in his chair, obviously thinking through the presentation Lloyd had just laid out. With that kind of set up, he thought, it just might work. Besides, he'd never been able to take care of his mama like he wanted to. A book deal would give her the security she needed to live her senior years in comfort, security she'd never had during her thirty years as a Metrobus dispatcher.

He was probably going to be behind bars for the rest of his life, so he might as well get something out of it. He looked at Lloyd.

"The only reason I'm even considering this is because of what you did for the city. You seem like a trustworthy guy. You guarantee that the interview won't run in your paper, or any other paper, until after a verdict has been rendered and I've been sentenced?"

"Yes, I guarantee it. I'll have to tell my editor that I got the interview recorded, but that you had this stipulation that we must honor. He'll have no choice but to go along."

"What if he forces you, tells you that you're fired if you don't give him the flash drive?"

"He'll be mad but, trust me, he won't fire me," said Lloyd, knowing that his clout at the *Ledger* had increased ten-fold in the last few days. "I'm too important to the paper right now. Besides, if he does fire me, I've got offers lined up from coast to coast from papers and magazines with larger circulations than the *Ledger*. I'll get it published one way or another."

Earl face broke out in a huge grin. "Okay, you've got a deal."

CHAPTER 31

Lloyd and Rosenfeld asked for permission to go out to Lloyd's car and then return to the facility. Although it was against regulations, Melvin made an exception and kept them both signed in on the visitors' roster. When they got to Lloyd's car, he retrieved his digital voice recorder out of the trunk and handed it to Rosenfeld, who put it in his briefcase. Attorneys were afforded wide latitude for bringing items into the facility when visiting their clients, so Rosenfeld could take a recording device inside whereas Lloyd could not.

When they returned to the private meeting area, Lloyd, Rosenfeld and Earl sat around the table. Rosenfeld placed the device in the center of the table and pressed *record*.

"Okay, Earl," said Lloyd, "why don't you tell me how you first met Keisha? How did the two of you hook up?"

"She was doing work study in one of the university offices. I was a salesman for one of the major phone providers, and I went to the office to see if I could get the university to switch phone services. I was trying to sign them up as a new client."

"I thought Keisha was cute, so I struck up a conversation. We talked for a few minutes, and I asked for her digits. She gave them to me right away."

Lloyd wanted to question Earl about the difference in their ages — the two of them were fifteen years apart. "She was quite a bit younger than you. Did you have any reservations about talking to her?"

"Nah, man. I like 'em young. These young girls will believe anything you tell 'em. Plus they usually don't have much experience sexually and you can really turn them out."

Lloyd decided to move on from that topic of discussion. "Okay, so you got her phone number and then what?"

"I waited a couple of days, and then I called her. I asked her to go out to lunch with me, and we hooked up the next day. I could tell she was feelin' me and I was laying the flattery on thick — complimenting her eyes and her smile. I told her I'd pick her up that Friday night and we'd go somewhere. She never asked any questions."

"So you got together that Friday and how did things progress? How did she end up moving in with you?"

"That Friday, I picked her up and took her to my place. I cooked us dinner, and I poured her a glass of wine. She said she didn't drink much, and I could tell she was getting relaxed. She kept drinking and I kept pouring. Pretty soon she was really buzzed.

"I kissed her, and she laid down and relaxed on the sofa. I kept kissing her and started taking off her clothes slowly. She didn't put up any resistance. And then I was inside her —tight and wet, man, tight and wet."

Lloyd didn't want to let Earl go too far down the road of sexual details. He didn't want Earl to be climbing the walls with sexual fantasies dominating his thoughts after they left. He was simply trying to get Earl comfortable talking about his relationship with Keisha. Lloyd would have to steer him back to the days leading up to the murder.

"So, after that you two started seeing each other regularly?"

"Yeah, man, we started kickin' it every day. I could tell she was falling for me, hard. I didn't have another lady at the time, so it was cool. When her mom found out about us, she wasn't too happy. Keisha was living in an apartment near the campus with two roommates, so her moms didn't know how much time we were spending together. After a couple of months, I asked her to move in with me and she did."

"How long did you two live together? Were things working out between you?"

"We lived together for about six months. At first, things were going pretty good. Keisha was in her classes during the day, and she would do a lot of the cooking and cleaning in the evenings. I had it made. She was always trying to make sure I was taken care of.

"But then she started being too clingy. Wanting to know my every move. She started calling me five or six times a day when I was at work. She was really getting on my nerves—nagging me. One thing I cannot stand is a bitch who nags.

"Then she started skipping class and following me. She suspected that I was cheating on her, seeing another woman behind her back. I wasn't; I just liked flirting with different females I encountered—hell, that's how I met her.

"On the day it happened, I came home from work and she lit into me, confronting me about some chick she saw me talking to earlier that day."

Lloyd interrupted him. "When you say 'on the day it happened,' you're talking about the murder, right?"

"Yeah, man. That's the day she made me really angry. She was up in my face, mouthing off about me hooking up with someone when I was supposed to be working. I didn't know what she was talking about at first.

"But then I remembered that I had an appointment earlier that day at the Allen Center downtown. The lady I was meeting with was going to lunch, and I walked out of the building with her. Keisha must have seen us talking outside in front of the building, but it was strictly business, I swear."

Lloyd was perplexed that Earl was feigning innocence about infidelity when he was locked up for a much graver offense—capital murder. "Go on, Earl. You say Keisha made you angry. Then what happened?"

"Well, when Keisha kept getting in my face, bobbing her neck from side to side—you know, the way sistas do when they're pissed off. Anyway, I kept warning her to back off, but she wouldn't listen. So I pushed her, not too hard, just enough to get her to back off.

"But she kept on hollering and screaming at me, and I had had enough. So I put my hands around her throat just to get her to shut up.

"I guess I had my hands there too long because when I let go, she fell to the floor and she wasn't breathing. I tried to do CPR, but it was too late. She was gone.

"I couldn't believe how fast it happened. I'm not a violent man, and I've never hit a woman in my life. You can ask Mr. Rosenfeld. I've never been arrested for anything but a traffic warrant."

Lloyd looked at Rosenfeld, who nodded, indicating that Earl was telling the truth. But Lloyd wanted to keep Earl talking until all of the details of the murder were included in the interview. "Once you realized Keisha was dead, did you call the police or notify anyone?"

"Nah, man, I panicked. I didn't want to go to jail for the rest of my life for something I did in the heat of passion. I know that when a female is killed, the most likely suspect is the husband or boyfriend, so I knew the cops would come looking for me. I had to think of a way to dispose of the body. Then I could tell her family that she went out of town to visit a friend, and I simply hadn't heard from her."

"I thought of putting the body in a dumpster across town, but as long as the authorities found her, I'd still be their number one suspect. That's when I thought about cutting up the body and putting each of the parts in different dumpsters."

Earl frowned. "But then they'd still be able to identify who she was with DNA evidence. I watch *CSI* and *Law and Order* so I know how forensic teams work," said Earl, smiling, obviously pleased with his knowledge of forensic science.

"The only way I could potentially destroy the DNA evidence was to burn the body parts. I felt bad about cutting Keisha up, but she was already dead and nothing was going to bring her back," Earl said as he shrugged.

"I used a hacksaw to cut up her body. I kept the body in the bathtub so I could rinse all of the blood down the drain. The cutting took me several hours and was messy as hell. But I had to keep going. I didn't want to end up in here.

"Anyway, I had to figure out a way to burn the parts without arousing suspicion. That's when I came up with the idea of burning them on my grill. I figured that if I included barbecue sauce and spice that they wouldn't smell any different than grilling hamburgers or hot dogs."

Lloyd interrupted. "Earl, did you really think no one would notice the stench of burning flesh?"

"I figured the smell would be a little different, but I thought the sauce would mask the odor. I must have been out of my mind. Maybe I was in shock," Earl mused.

"So, once you started doing the barbecuing, what happened?"

"I was doing the barbecuing on my apartment's patio balcony, and when I had finished with her arms and legs, the smell was so overwhelming that I had to cover my nose and mouth with a bandana. Still, I was gagging, like I was going to vomit. I tried spraying Febreze and Lysol, which helped some, but the smell didn't completely go away.

"Then I heard the fire truck sirens. Someone must have called the fire department about the smell."

"Yes, Earl," Lloyd interjected, "a couple of people from your apartment complex called 911 about what they thought were toxic fumes."

"Well, once I heard the sirens, I really got nervous. I turned off the gas on the grill so the fire would go out. Then I lowered the hood on the grill so the smoke wouldn't travel from my patio and lead the firemen to me.

"I put the charred remains in two Hefty bags, along with the rest of Keisha's body that I had in the bathtub. Because the grill was on the patio, the fire department couldn't pinpoint the exact location of the fumes. They knocked on each apartment door in the vicinity of the odor and, when they got to my place, I was very quiet and didn't answer."

"Once the coast was clear, I waited until after dark and put the Hefty bags in the trunk of my car. I drove about twenty miles to the landfill on the outskirts of town and dumped the bags there. I figured the bags would be buried underneath piles of garbage dumped by the waste management companies and that Keisha's body would decompose before anything was found."

"But a couple of days later the cops had some blood hounds sniffing at the landfill and they found the Hefty bags. I'm not sure why the dogs were there."

Lloyd was aware of the circumstances leading up to the dog searches. "Earl, the dogs are taken to the landfill for random searches about once a month. You're not the first person who has tried to hide a dead body at a landfill. So, a few years ago, the Harris County Commissioners contracted a company to conduct the random sniff searches. They've discovered several dead bodies since the periodic searches began."

"I guess that explains it. Anyway, when Keisha's mother filed the missing person's report, she gave the cops a strand of hair from one of Keisha's hair brushes. From the hair sample, they were able to match the DNA from Keisha's body.

"After that, it only took them a few hours to get a judge to sign a search warrant for my apartment. Even though I had cleaned the bathtub thoroughly, there were traces of Keisha's blood on the tile and faucet. They arrested me while the lab boys were still in my apartment taking samples, and they charged me with capital murder."

"Earl, do you have any regrets?"

"What do you think, man? I'm going to be locked up for the rest of my life."

"What I mean is, if you could go back and change things, what would you have done differently?"

"I would have just left the apartment when Keisha was going off on me. I've never put my hands on a woman in my life. I had no idea that a person could be killed that easily. I really didn't mean to do it."

"Anything else?"

"After it happened, I should have called the cops and turned myself in. The fact that I didn't and that I tried to dispose of the body in a heinous fashion is going to make the judge go a lot harsher with his punishment.

"People could understand me accidentally choking Keisha in anger. But me cutting up the body—it would be impossible to find twelve jurors who could relate to taking that kind of action. In the end, I got caught anyway."

Lloyd hit the *stop* button on the recorder. "Well, Earl, I think this will do it. You can be sure that the flash drive containing the recording of this interview will be placed in safekeeping until after your sentencing hearing."

"Do you know when the plea bargain process will be complete?" Lloyd asked Rosenfeld. "What sort of time frame are we looking at? My editor is going to ask me, so I need to have an answer."

"First, the prosecutor is going to drag things out so he can garner some headlines. The public is outraged by this case, and rightly so, Earl. The prosecutor can't appear to be giving in to you too easily," said Rosenfeld.

"We've asked for twenty years; they've hinted that they want a minimum of thirty years to life. My guess is that we'll end up with about twenty-five years as long as you allocute—that means you fully confess to the details of the crime. They'll take about a month to make their offer. The whole process, including sentencing, should be completed within about sixty days. Earl, you should be prepared to serve at least fifteen years of whatever sentence you get, if they knock off time for good behavior."

"So that's it, Earl. Rosenfeld and I will go straight to the bank to set up the safe deposit box as soon as we leave here." Lloyd offered Earl his hand, and Earl shook it. "When the interview runs in the paper, I'll make sure Rosenfeld gets a few copies that he can give you. And I hope that whatever time you have to spend behind bars is used productively."

"Thanks, Lloyd. I enjoyed meeting you, but I wish it was under different circumstances."

CHAPTER 32

Lloyd and Rosenfeld left the jail and decided to take separate cars to the bank to set up the safe deposit box. Lloyd got his cell phone out of the trunk before heading to the bank branch that he had in mind, which was close to the *Ledger*'s office downtown. He checked his missed calls and saw that he had three calls from Ed, who he knew was going to be anxious at first, then livid, when Lloyd told him about the arrangements. He pressed the call button to dial Ed back. Better to go ahead and get the call over with. Ed answered right away.

"Ed, it's Lloyd. I got the interview."

"What? I don't believe it," Ed said excitedly. "You mean he gave you a date when he agreed to do it?"

"No, Ed. I conducted the actual interview with him at the jail with his lawyer present. That's why you couldn't reach me on my cell phone."

Ed was animated, elated beyond measure. "You've got to be kidding. Why would he and his lawyer agree to do it?"

"Well, there is one catch."

"I knew it. What sort of catch?"

"I had to agree to not publish the interview until after he's sentenced. That's the only way he would do it."

"Okay, I can understand that, and that's no problem. Bring the tape in so I can listen to it."

"That's part of the catch, Ed. It's on a digital data card but I don't have it."

Ed's was first exasperated, then infuriated. "You mean you gave it to his lawyer? Of all the idiotic things I've ever heard . . . "

"Calm down, Ed. His lawyer doesn't have it either."

"Then where the hell is it?"

"It's in a safe deposit box, and his lawyer and I have to be at the bank together in order to open the box and get the flash drive. You should be happy, Ed. We got the exclusive interview."

"Don't tell me how I should feel, Lloyd, because you don't have a clue. Furthermore, you have neither the authority nor the invitation to make those kinds of executive decisions at the *Ledger*. This stuff is getting out of hand. At what bank is the safe deposit box located?"

"I'm sorry, Ed. I can't tell you. I promised Griffin and his attorney that the information would be kept strictly confidential. I gave them my solemn oath, and I have to keep my word."

Ed was shouting at the top of his lungs now. "Listen, Mister Integrity, there's a right way and a wrong way to do things in the field. You can't hold things back from your boss and expect to keep your job. Now bring me that flash drive."

"I'm sorry, Ed. I couldn't bring it now, even if I wanted to."

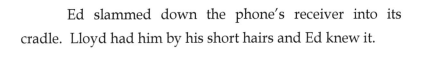

Ed slammed down the phone's receiver into its cradle. Lloyd had him by his short hairs and Ed knew it.

CHAPTER 33

It was after 4:00 p.m., and Lloyd had spent the entire day fielding media interviews in the morning and meeting with Griffin in the afternoon. He was mentally and emotionally exhausted and decided to go home. Going to the office was definitely out of the question. He wanted to avoid a confrontation with Ed until he had time to cool off, and by tomorrow he would be easier to deal with.

When he arrived at home, Stephanie was already there. Since school dismissed at three fifteen, she was usually home by four thirty. She was sitting at the kitchen table reading a book she had started the night before.

"What are you doing home so early, hon? Is everything okay?"

"Yeah, I just finished up early and decided to come on home instead of hanging around at the office. Where's Bria?"

"She stayed after school for a meeting of the yearbook committee. She's always on the go. I guess we're getting a trial run of how the empty nest will feel when she leaves for college."

Stephanie looked up at Lloyd curiously. "But there's something you're not telling me. What is it?"

"I had a minor disagreement with Ed. Actually, it's a major disagreement, not a minor one, but he'll get over it."

"That seems to be happening a lot lately. Do you want to talk about it?"

"Things are starting to move awfully fast, Steph. The past few weeks have been surreal. I almost feel like I'm in the Twilight Zone. People recognize me on the street, I've been on nearly every television news program in America, and I'm going to be on the cover of *Time* magazine's next issue."

"Those are all good things, Lloyd. You've been working hard your whole life. Now your hard work is beginning to pay off."

"My career advancement seems to be creating a tremendous amount of friction with Ed. He used to be able to intimidate me, but not anymore. I think that's what angers him the most."

"Doesn't he realize that the work you're doing benefits the paper?"

"Yes, but he's been accustomed to total domination over me for the past ten years. I'm not sure he can relate to me any other way."

"Well, he's your boss, not your overseer. I don't want you to be stressed out when you go to work every day. With the options you have available to you now, you can start putting feelers out elsewhere. When you find a new position, you'll be able to work at a media outlet where the dynamics are completely different."

Lloyd could always count on Stephanie to watch his back. "There are a couple of projects I'm working on that I'd like to see through to completion, so I need to figure out how to keep Ed sufficiently satisfied until then. That reminds me of something. I went to the Harris County Jail today and interviewed Earl Allen Griffin."

"The guy who killed that poor girl and tried to roast her body on the grill? Oh my God, Lloyd. Did he appear to be insane because that's the only reason I can think of that someone would do something like that? What did he say?"

"He confessed to everything that happened in complete detail. And you know, Steph, you can't reveal this to anybody, not even your closest friends. I know you don't repeat things I tell you about work, but this has to be kept strictly confidential. The news on TV made it sound like the guy's a cannibal."

"You know I won't repeat it, Lloyd. Does he seem to be mentally unbalanced?"

"No, Steph. Actually, it seems more like he just lost control and killed her by accident. The whole grill thing was a bizarre attempt to cover up his crime. Right now his lawyer is negotiating a plea bargain, so I agreed not to publish the interview until his sentencing hearing is done. But I need you to do something for me."

"In relation to Earl Allen Griffin? What could I possibly do?"

"I put the tape of the interview in a safe deposit box at Chase Bank downtown on Bagby Street. Here's the receipt," he said as he handed the bank form to Stephanie.

"Griffin's lawyer has the key, and to get the tape we both have to be present at the bank. When I filled out the paperwork, I listed you as the joint owner of the box. That way, in case something happens to me, Griffin's story can still be published."

Stephanie's apprehension was visible, and her anxiety level shot through the roof. "Lloyd, you're scaring me. Have you been threatened or something? Or is this just a precaution?"

Lloyd attempted to relieve Stephanie's fears. "No, of course I haven't been threatened. I'm just covering my bases in case. Don't worry," Lloyd said as he pulled Stephanie toward him and gave her a hug.

"Besides, I got a text message from Hamisi today."

Stephanie stepped back and looked up at Lloyd. "You did? What did it say?"

"It said, 'The truth must be protected at all costs.' I just want to have a backup plan because you never know what might happen."

Stephanie put the safe deposit receipt in her skirt pocket. "Okay, Lloyd. I'll put this in a safe place. And I'm going to pray that God keeps you from all hurt, harm and danger."

CHAPTER 34

The *Time* magazine interview and photo shoot went well. The edition with Lloyd on the cover was on newsstands a few days later with the headline, "Can Lloyd Palmer Change the Face of Journalism?" *Time* had portrayed Lloyd as a modern-day crusader, willing to do whatever it took to uncover the truth. He was compared to respected journalists of an earlier era, like Edward R. Murrow and Walter Cronkite.

For Lloyd, it was a mixed blessing. He was well aware of the media's penchant for building up individuals to be larger than life one day, and then exposing their foibles and cutting them down to size the next. He'd have to be careful to keep his ego in check since he could very well be a hero today and a villain tomorrow.

He'd received congratulatory calls about the *Time* magazine cover from too many people to count—from his parents; extended family; his best friend, Ron; old running buddies, long-lost friends, and his peers in the industry. Ed had even expressed some words of encouragement, albeit reluctantly. After all, because of Lloyd, the *Ledger* was once again receiving the type of free, positive publicity that money could not buy.

The day after the Griffin interview, Lloyd had gone into Ed's office to reassure him that the circumstances surrounding the storage of the data card would work out in the *Ledger*'s favor in the end; that it was the only way Griffin would agree to do the interview and that Lloyd would handle the details in the *Ledger*'s best interest.

Ed appeared to be satisfied with that although Lloyd could tell Ed still felt that his authority had been usurped. Lloyd thought he might need to start looking over his shoulder with more intensity. He could only guess what Ed might do in retaliation since, at this juncture, firing him was probably out of the question.

Lloyd had taken a couple of days of personal leave after the *Time* photo shoot for some much needed relaxation. He had been working nearly nonstop for the past two weeks, and he need to rest and recharge. Now he was on his way to have dinner with Professor Gastalt to obtain as much information as he could about the Lembas.

They had agreed to meet at seven o'clock at a restaurant near Rice University called The Raven Grill. Since the two of them had never met, they decided to wait out front to make it easier to locate each other. When Lloyd pulled into the parking lot, he noticed a man with a gray beard and wearing glasses standing out front who resembled Gastalt from the photos Lloyd had seen online.

After Lloyd parked, he walked toward the entrance and introduced himself. "Dr. Gastalt?" Lloyd asked as he reached for the professor's hand.

Gastalt smiled broadly. "Lloyd Palmer, it's a pleasure to meet you. I recognize you from the T.V. interviews I've seen. Good job, by the way, on getting to the bottom of the Pauley kidnapping. Are you ready to go inside?"

"Yes, I'm starving, so let's go eat."

When the hostess greeted them, they requested a table near the rear so they wouldn't disturb others around them with their discussion. As they walked toward their table, Lloyd received an alert of an incoming text message on his cell phone. It was from Hamisi.

Don't let the spotlight compromise your principles and your quest for the truth.

Hamisi always seemed to be at least two steps ahead of him, as if he were tracking Lloyd's every move and could see into his future. He had the uncanny ability to say just the right thing at just the right time.

Once Lloyd and the professor were seated and ordered their beverages, Lloyd was the first one to break the ice. "I really appreciate your agreeing to meet with me, Professor. I've completed a lot of my research, and your knowledge will add nicely to the information I have already obtained."

"As I mentioned to you, I've met a member of the Lemba tribe here in Houston, and he piqued my interest. I had never heard of them before that."

"Yes, I remember you saying that. What was the gentleman's name?"

"I can't tell you that, Professor. I promised him that I wouldn't reveal his identity."

"Ah, yes, some of them can be quite secretive. Can you describe him?"

"I don't think there would be any harm in that. He was of medium height, very dark skinned, but the pure African sort of coloring, if you know what I mean."

"What about his facial features?"

Lloyd thought for a moment. "Well, his face was somewhat elongated, as was his nose. His nose is broad like most people of African descent, but it's both broad and elongated."

"What about his clothing? Did he have any unusual garments?"

"When I first met him at his apartment, he had on a head covering that looked like a Jewish yarmulke."

"Anything else?"

"He had a shawl around his shoulders that had the Star of David with an elephant in the center."

The professor sat up straight, rubbing his right hand on his chin. "He's a Lemba alright. Well, I'll be damned."

"What can you tell me about them from the time you spent with them in Africa?"

"They're a very cloistered group with a lot of rituals and traditions, some of which can only be observed by other Lemba. Just like the Jews in America, they don't eat pork, they perform circumcisions, and they observe Sabbath on the seventh day of the week. They also have an oral history which dates back thousands of years, to antiquity in fact."

Lloyd nodded his head in agreement. "My contact here in Houston told me the same things. Is it true that they can trace their roots back to Moses' brother Aaron in the book of Exodus?"

"Their oral history certainly suggests this and there has also been DNA to support this assertion. But they seem to be less interested in publicity than in preserving the sanctity of their customs and traditions. In fact, they shun the spotlight. That's why I'm surprised that you were able to get your friend to talk."

"I met him purely by accident, I assure you," said Lloyd. "He seems to have taken a liking to me, almost as if I was his own son. He told me that his sons were still in Zimbabwe, so maybe by taking me under his wing he can still feel close to them, in a way. What more can you tell me?"

"They say they built the ancient city of Great Zimbabwe, the ruins of which are still standing."

"I've done quite a bit of research on my own and I know about the DNA, the Great City and even Senna and Pusela," Lloyd told him. "I was hoping you could tell me something that may not be part of the historical research; something that you perhaps discovered while you were living among them."

Professor Gastalt paused, then said, "Well, this isn't necessarily something for publication, but I'm pretty sure they have an enforcement squad."

"An enforcement squad?" asked Lloyd. Hamisi hadn't said anything about the Lembas' style of policing nor their concepts of justice. "What kind of enforcement squad? What does this squad actually do?"

"Every tribe, group, country, whatever has a system of defending itself. That is, if they plan to survive," replied the professor. "The Lemba are no different."

"Do you mean like the Japanese ninjas or samurai? What's this enforcement squad called?"

"I'm not sure if they have a formal name, but only a select few from each region qualify. According to one of the Lemba elders, the squad members go through years of special training and are able to break nearly every bone in a man's body with their bare hands."

Lloyd was intrigued. "Wow. I doubt my contact had those types of skills. He seemed like the sort of man who wouldn't lift a finger against anyone."

"Don't let his appearance deceive you. These guys are highly skilled and can infiltrate a situation in a matter of seconds. I've never actually seen the squad in operation, but I'm told that they operate in stealth fashion. If you're one of their targets, you never see them coming, and death comes quickly."

The professor bent down underneath the table and retrieved a manila folder out of his satchel, which he handed to Lloyd.

"Anyway, here's a copy of some of my research on the Lemba during my months with them in Zimbabwe. This should help you with your article. Do right by them, okay?"

"I want nothing more than to introduce the Lemba to the world in the best possible way," Lloyd assured him. "I give you my word on that. Now, let's eat."

CHAPTER 35

Once Lloyd got home, he spent his evening refining the article, combining the information he already had with the research documents he received from the professor. There were some of Gastalt's statements he could use, but he still needed some first-hand statements from an actual Lemba to add credibility to his article. He doubted Ed or any editor would accept it without that central, critical piece of data. And he also needed the all important "art" – a term in the newspaper business that meant a photograph of the subject featured in the article.

Lloyd could not quote nor take a photo of Hamisi; his new Lemba friend had been emphatic about that. But if he could get in touch with the head of the Lemba Cultural Society, he was hoping he could convince the guy to make his statements on the record.

He wanted to contact Hamisi and ask him about the enforcement squad, but he wanted to reserve his communications with Hamisi until there was something really important to say. He had a feeling that if he attempted to communicate with his new friend too frequently, Hamisi would simply disappear.

Lloyd looked at the clock and couldn't believe it was nearly 2:00 a.m. He had completely lost track of time; totally absorbed in the work he was doing. He had to get up to go to work in less than five hours, and he was fairly exhausted although his mind was still engaged, still churning with ideas.

But he decided to go to bed; otherwise, he wouldn't have the energy to focus at work the next day. Since he had been out of the office for a few days, he didn't want to risk dozing off at his desk while waiting for Ed to give him an assignment. Ed was probably still pissed off at him—no need to pour salt into the wound.

The next day when he arrived at the office, he had a few notes of congratulations on his desk from co-workers. A couple of them were people who'd barely spoken to him in the past. What a difference a *Time* magazine cover made!

While he was checking his office voice mail, Charles walked up and sat on his desk. When Lloyd was done writing down his messages, he hung up the phone.

"So man, how does it feel?" asked Charles.

"How does what feel?"

"How does it feel to be famous?"

Lloyd laughed. "First of all, I'm not famous. After a few days, this will all blow over, and I'll go back to being a mild-mannered reporter again like Clark Kent."

"Don't laugh. Clark Kent went into a phone booth and emerged as Superman, which is basically what you did with the Pauley story. I'm real proud of you, man, and thanks for bringing me along for the ride."

"You had my back, Charles, and that means a lot. Thanks for being a true friend," said Lloyd, as he gave Charles a fist bump.

"By the way, did you hear about the special section the *Ledger* is doing for Holy Week?"

Lloyd wondered what in the world the paper would be featuring for Easter and Lent, unless it involved a travel tour guide to the Holy Land. During this time of year, the paper made lots of advertising dollars from retail stores trying to sell all types of Easter paraphernalia: Church outfits for the kids, hats for the ladies, and more chocolate Easter bunnies than could be easily counted.

Some folks only went to church one Sunday of the year and that was on Easter. And even folks who didn't attend church purchased Easter eggs, egg-dying kits, candy and baskets used for Easter egg hunts and rolls. The day represented a tremendous bonanza for apparel and discount stores, and with subscription revenues shrinking rapidly, the *Ledger* depended on holiday ad dollars for its very existence.

Ed tended to steer clear from delving into controversial religious topics for fear of offending one denomination or another or, worse, being sued by atheist fringe groups for daring to mention religion or a deity at all. Lloyd was mystified. "What possessed Ed to venture off in that direction?"

"I think he's trying to piggyback off of the Museum of Fine Arts exhibit that's in town. There are some religious artifacts on display right now, including the Dead Sea Scrolls that are on loan from the Israel Museum. Someone from the Lifestyle section planted the seed and Ed decided to run with it. I don't know all the details, but apparently they plan to include several articles and try for some local tie-ins. Check with Ed on it."

As Charles was talking, Lloyd's mind was churning. He was thinking about how he could position his feature about the Lemba for inclusion in the special section. These special sections tended to have a longer shelf life with readers and often received recognition beyond the city or even the state. He then realized he had begun daydreaming and had lost focus on what Charles was saying.

"Hey, man, are you listening?" asked Charles, snapping his fingers in front of Lloyd's face as Lloyd emerged from his self-induced trance.

"Oh, I'm sorry, Charles. I was thinking about something."

"Obviously."

"I'll check with Ed, but I'm hoping he's not still pissed at me. He was pretty steamed at me last week—about everything."

"He'll get over it, Lloyd. In fact, I'm sure it's already blown over. Just remember that he's an editor first, and he'll be most interested in putting out the best product he can from an editorial standpoint."

"Are you sure about that? You have a lot more confidence in Ed's ability to put personal issues aside than I do. But thanks for pulling my coat about this. I'll talk to Ed about it soon."

CHAPTER 36

Lloyd didn't have a lot of time to develop a game plan before Ed called him into his office. Lloyd figured he could drop a hint with Ed about the Holy Week section so he could gauge whether or not he should push further. After all, he didn't know whether or not his article about the Lemba would even fit with what Ed was planning. Things were still quite tense between them.

Ed's office door was open, and Lloyd sat down in one of the two chairs facing Ed's desk. "What's up, Ed?"

"There's an accident that happened a few minutes ago, and I want you to cover it. Close the door, will 'ya?"

"Okay, Ed," Lloyd said, and rose from his chair. As he grabbed the door's frame to push it closed, Audrey walked past and blew him a seductive kiss. Lloyd closed the door and rolled his eyes. Good grief, he thought. Audrey never quit.

"A five-year-old boy was just hit by a car at the Money Mart on the North Beltway," said Ed, before Lloyd could sit down. "I've put you on this one because, since you've become the public face of the guy who solved the Pauley kidnapping, the public sees you as credible, especially when it comes to stories about crimes against children. You'll need to leave right away."

"Wait a minute, Ed. Did the kid get hurt? What hospital did they take him to?"

"Unfortunately, he was pronounced dead at the scene. A real tragedy; apparently the mother left him in the parking lot, as a way of teaching him a lesson. There's also at least one eyewitness. That's about all the info I've got. Now, get going."

"Okay, Ed. I'm leaving. But I do have one quick question."

"Shoot. What is it?"

"Charles told me the paper is publishing a special religious section for Holy Week."

Ed was writing something on a pad and kept right on writing. He barely looked up. "So, what about it?"

"I was wondering what it's all about exactly."

Ed raised his head from the notes that had been occupying his attention. "Why would you want to know about that?"

"Oh, I'm just curious." Lloyd had to be careful. He didn't want Ed to get suspicious.

"If you must know, it's about local religious groups and their connection to Biblical history. One of the religion reporters found a Houston area synagogue that claims to have dust from the Wall of Jericho in its repository. And there's an Episcopal church in Tomball that says it has some artifacts from Jesus' last supper with his disciples. We're using those examples, along with the Museum of Fine Arts exhibit, as the basis of a religion piece."

"Sounds interesting. Well, I'm heading out to the Money Mart now. Hopefully, the witness will still be there but if not, I'll get her info from law enforcement. I'll check in later."

Lloyd smiled as he left Ed's office. His plan was now in full effect.

CHAPTER 37

Money Mart stores had sprung up all over the state of Texas. These bargain merchandisers advertised that they would beat any competitor's prices for standard household goods, from paper towels to flat screen TVs. Because of their cheap prices, these sprawling megastores, with their aisles and aisles of made-in-China merchandise, attracted people from all backgrounds. Low-income families headed by single mothers, stressed out from the pressures of raising children alone on limited resources, were some of Money Mart's most frequent customers.

Such was the case for poor Tommy Ray Samuels' mother, the woman who left her five-year-old in the Money Mart parking lot because he was walking too slowly and she was in a hurry. Lloyd learned this from Jennifer Green, the woman who was exiting Money Mart and on her way to her car with her packages when the horrible accident happened.

Lloyd had arrived at the scene about fifteen minutes after leaving the office, and Green was still on the premises, according to Sheriff Martin, the officer Lloyd spoke with when he arrived. Martin pointed to Green, who was sitting on a bench outside the Money Mart Garden Center.

"She's still pretty shaken up," said Martin. "She saw the whole thing happen."

"What about the mother? Do you know anything about her?"

"Well, she was pretty hysterical when we took her into custody. About the only coherent information we could get out of her was that she lived in the Mountain Pines Trailer Park over on Cutten Road."

Lloyd took out his notepad and wrote down some notes. "What happened to the driver of the vehicle?"

"He was taken to the precinct to give a statement, but I don't think he'll be charged with anything," replied Martin. "From all accounts, he wasn't exceeding the speed limit. He just couldn't see the little tike until it was too late. It's a damn shame, too. The boy's name was Tommy Ray Samuels."

Lloyd wrote down some more details, then looked in the direction of the witness, who was sitting on the bench with her head in her hands. "Okay, thanks Sheriff Martin," he said, as he walked over to the bench where Green was sitting. When he got there, he placed his hand on her shoulder.

"Ms. Green, may I speak with you a moment?"

She turned and looked up at him with reddened, swollen eyes. She'd obviously been crying for quite some time.

"Who are you? A detective?" she asked, between sniffles.

"No m'am. I'm Lloyd Palmer with the *Houston Ledger*. Do you mind if I sit down?"

"No, it's okay. I guess you're here about the little boy."

"Yes, m'am. The sheriff said you saw the whole thing."

"I still can't believe it happened. The whole thing unfolded before my very eyes, like it . . . like it was in slow motion, you know? What kind of mother leaves her child in a Money Mart parking lot?" she asked no one in particular, as she broke down into uncontrollable sobs.

Lloyd patted her on her back to comfort her. Once she recovered, she looked ahead as if she were reliving the accident, shaking her head in disbelief.

"Can you tell me what happened?" Lloyd asked gently. "Did you know the boy or his mother?"

"No, my being here at the same time was just a heartbreaking coincidence. I actually wish I hadn't been here because it will be a long time before I can get the images of what happened out of my head."

"Sheriff Martin told me you were walking to your car," Lloyd said, half question and half statement of fact, prodding her along, but not pushing so she'd shut down completely.

"Well, I had just gone through the checkout line and exited the double doors over there," she said, pointing to the sliding doors nearest them. "I was pushing my shopping cart toward my car, which was parked about ten cars away from the entrance."

"While I was walking, a woman and her two children passed me on my right. She had a young woman with her; I presume it was her friend. The little boy was walking slower than they were, you know, being a little stubborn. He wasn't throwing a tantrum or anything, but you could tell he was walking slowly on purpose."

Lloyd didn't interrupt because she obviously wanted to get all of the details off her chest, perhaps in hopes of easing her own conscience.

"She was yelling at him, telling him to walk faster or she would leave him. Then he stopped walking completely. But the mom said something like, 'Okay. Be that way. I'm gonna leave you out here by yourself. I'm sick of this stubborn shit.'"

"Excuse me, Mr. Palmer. I don't use profanity at all. But when she said this to her son, it shocked me. That's no way to talk to a child, your own or anyone else's."

"What happened next, Ms. Green?"

"The rest is so horrible, it's hard to repeat," she said, and sobbed again. Lloyd let her take her time. He was trying to digest it all himself.

"I've already told this once to the sheriff." She took a couple of deep breaths.

"I had put my bags in the trunk of my car and had just put the trunk down. After she said that part about the boy being stubborn, she said to her little girl and the lady who was with them, 'Come on. Let's go inside.' And she walked right into the store and left him in the parking lot."

"I just stood there for a minute at my car, watching, expecting her to turn around and come back. But, not only did she not come back, she didn't even *look* back. She kept walking as if he wasn't there. She went inside the sliding entrance doors and then the doors closed, which meant she wasn't even near enough to keep the doors open."

"That's when the boy started walking slowly toward the door. I knew instinctively that it was dangerous, that a disaster was unfolding, but the mother never came out. I started running toward him to catch his little hand. I was about fifty feet away, and then I picked up my pace. I tried to catch up, but I didn't reach him in time."

"Just when he got to the driveway—you know the two-lane part that you walk across before you get to the entrance—he started running toward the door. That's when the car hit him. He was so small, I guess the driver didn't see him in time. I knew he was dead the way his little body hit the pavement and the car's front tire rolled over him. I just can't believe it," she said, sobbing again.

Lloyd sat there silently, continuing to pat her back. He reached in his bag and offered her some tissues — the same packet of tissues that Stephanie had given him and that he had used to unearth the Pauley boy's body — which she accepted. She blew her nose and dabbed at her eyes.

"When the car hit him, the boy's mother let out a shrill scream. I can still hear it ringing in my ears. She fell to her knees next to the boy's body, holding him in her arms, calling his name over and over again. She was beside herself with grief, but it was too late. The sheriff arrested her, but there's nothing they can do to her in jail that would be worse than the torment of living with her son's death. That child would still be alive if not for her stupidity."

"Ms. Green, I hope you're not blaming yourself for what happened to Tommy. That was the little boy's name. Tommy Lee Samuels."

"I know. His mother screamed, 'Tommy, wake up,' more times than I can count. I can't help but feeling that if I had run just a little faster, or if I had started running sooner, I could have gotten to him in time."

Lloyd tried his best to comfort her. "You had no way of knowing his mother was going to leave him outside. You were probably too stunned to move. You did more than most people would have done when you ran towards him. Don't blame yourself."

Green looked at Lloyd and blew her nose again. "I appreciate you saying that, Mr. Palmer. My heart just hurts right now."

"Ms. Green, can I do anything for you? Can I get Sheriff Martin to take you home?"

"That won't be necessary. My husband is on his way to pick me up. I was on my lunch break from work when this happened, but I let them know that I wasn't coming back to the office today. I wouldn't be able to concentrate on much of anything anyway."

CHAPTER 38

A week had passed and Lloyd's days at the *Ledger* were essentially back to normal. He traveled around Houston and reported on the stories Ed assigned him, but it was clear that his stature had been raised. When he arrived at most locations, more often than not his interview subjects recognized him. Some people even asked for autographs or wanted their pictures taken with him, which he obliged.

Lloyd had spent so many years in obscurity as an anonymous reporter that he never expected to be in the limelight. At least his name was associated with something positive. As Hamisi said, most of the names mentioned in the *Ledger* belonged to people who had experienced something negative in their lives—either tragedies or scandals.

Lloyd hadn't heard from Hamisi in more than two weeks. He thought about making contact with him via e-mail, but he didn't want to be a nuisance or spook him. He was afraid that if he pushed Hamisi too hard, he'd disappear completely. Lloyd didn't want to risk that. He'd have to be patient.

Since he had finished his article about the Lemba, he felt the time was right to approach Ed and get approval for the paper's Holy Week section. In fact, he felt confident when he walked toward Ed's office that morning, expecting a thumbs-up with little resistance.

Ed's office door was closed, so Lloyd knocked first and waited for a response.

"Come on in," Ed said, and when Lloyd opened the door, Wilson Cox, the paper's executive vice president, was seated across from him.

"Good to see you, Lloyd," Cox said. "I don't have to tell you what a great job you're doing with your reporting. I don't know why you didn't come to our attention sooner. How long have you been working for the *Ledger*?

"Ten years, sir. And thanks for the compliment."

"Ten years? Are you kidding? Ed, where have you been hiding him all this time?"

Ed grimaced. "Lloyd's been a beat reporter covering basic traffic accidents, murders, a few political stories, Wilson. Until the Pauley kidnapping, he'd always worked on routine stuff. But I'm glad the two of you got a chance to meet," Ed replied disingenuously.

Ed was lying through his teeth. The last thing he wanted was for Lloyd to have Wilson Cox's ear. A chummy relationship between the two of them could prove to be disastrous. But he had to play the role of the proud editor.

Cox rose from his chair to leave and shook Lloyd's hand. "Great job, Lloyd. Feel free to call me anytime if you have any ideas or concerns. Here's my card, and my cell phone number is on the back."

"Thank you, sir. I'll keep that in mind," Lloyd said, as he smiled to himself, at Cox and at Ed. He couldn't have hoped for a better development if he had planned it himself.

After Cox left, Ed asked, "What do you need, Lloyd?"

"I wanted to talk to you about that Holy Week section you're publishing in a couple of weeks. I have an article I've been working on that would be perfect for it."

Ed was dubious. "Really? You've never done exposé or feature story writing. You've always been strictly a beat reporter."

"I know, but I recently became aware of a little-known religious sect and I decided to try my hand at writing a feature story. I'd like to talk to you about it if you have a few minutes."

Ed reared back in his chair with his arms crossed. His body language told the story: He was completely close-minded about everything Lloyd was about to say. But Lloyd knew Ed would at least act as though he was open to his ideas. After all, Lloyd could pick up the phone and call *the* Wilson Cox, whose great-grandfather had started the *Ledger* in the early 1900s.

"Okay, make it quick," Ed snapped.

"My article is about a tribe known as the Lemba. They can trace their roots to Aaron, Moses' brother in the Bible, and it's been verified through DNA."

"A tribe? A tribe from where?"

"From Africa, from Zimbabwe to be exact."

"Zimbabwe? Lloyd, I don't see how this is relevant to the section we're doing."

"But you see, Ed, it is relevant because I met one of the members of the tribe right here in Houston. These are actual people with a rich and verifiable history."

"How do you know it's verifiable?"

"How do you know the synagogue's claim that they have dust from the Wall of Jericho is real? Can they provide proof? And, if not, why are you running an article about them in the paper?"

Ed's face reddened, and he had the expression that usually preceded a meltdown. "Lloyd, what right do you have to question my authority? What you're describing sounds preposterous. In all my born days, I've never heard about any African tribe that has anything to do with the Bible."

"Ed, do you go to church?"

"Once in a while. So what?"

Lloyd seized on Ed's obvious shortcomings as a Biblical scholar. "And do you ever read the Bible?"

"Occasionally, but it's common knowledge . . ."

"I'm sorry to interrupt you, Ed, but if you don't go to church and you rarely read the Bible, how do you know what's in it?"

Ed was fuming, and flummoxed. He knew that Lloyd was at least partially correct, but he refused to acquiesce. "I don't have to read the Bible to know that what you're talking about is malarkey."

"Did you know that at least a portion of the Garden of Eden was located in Africa, specifically in Ethiopia?"

"What the hell are you talking about?"

"It's right there in the book of Genesis, but since you don't read the Bible, you wouldn't know that," Lloyd said with smug sarcasm. He knew he was crossing a line with Ed, pushing his buttons, getting under his skin, but he didn't care. As far as he was concerned, this was a man-to-man conversation, and Ed just happened to be the man who authorized his paychecks.

"Dammit, I've had enough of this, Lloyd, and enough of you. There's not going to be any article on the Mumba tribe and that's final."

"It's Lemba, Ed, not Mumba. Would you mind giving me a reason why you won't even read my article?"

"Because we can't publish something that farfetched. Our readers would be lighting up the switchboard and cancelling their subscriptions, asking if we'd lost our damn minds. And it's not verifiable. Can you produce this fella you say you met?"

"Ed, he's a confidential source, and you know I can't divulge his identity. Besides, the *New York Times* published an article about the Lemba over a decade ago; there's also been a book about them . . . ."

"This isn't New York, and we don't do things like that in Texas. I still haven't forgotten how you held back the recording of Earl Allen Griffin's murder confession. Now I'm done talking about this. Get out of here, Lloyd, before you really make me angry."

At first, Lloyd was going to continue to press Ed further. But he thought it best to retreat now, regroup and perhaps approach the subject from another angle before the deadline. As he opened Ed's door and walked out of his office, Lloyd's cell phone vibrated, indicating an incoming text message: *Watch, fight and pray.* It was from Hamisi.

CHAPTER 39

Ed had just about reached his limit with Lloyd. There were some things he couldn't abide, and one of them was an insubordinate reporter working for him. Lloyd's feature story idea came out of nowhere. Even though Ed hated to admit that it sounded like a fascinating idea in many ways, the *Ledger* simply couldn't publish something like that. It was too much of a stretch from people's core religious beliefs. He'd have the entire religious community on his back: the Catholics, the Protestants, the Jews—even the black churches would be uncomfortable opening such a can of worms.

The Holy Week section was supposed to reinforce the religious concepts that were already common knowledge, not present some new information that would make a large segment of the Houston population uncomfortable or even irate. And for what? People were going to stick to what they'd believed all their lives—no matter what the *Ledger* printed. He couldn't afford for the *Ledger* to become a laughing stock over something that, in the final analysis, wouldn't change one person's mind.

But he didn't think he could convince Lloyd to completely drop the matter either. Lloyd's newfound obstinance was unmistakable.

And Ed definitely couldn't take a chance on getting Wilson Cox involved. Who could predict how Cox would respond? The blue-blooded, old-money prick might just side with Lloyd.

He thought about contacting Bubba. If Bubba pulled one of his dirty tricks on Lloyd, that could scare him enough to get him to back off. That was a risky proposition, but he might not have any other choice.

But, on second thought, it would be better to get someone to talk to Lloyd and bring him back to his senses. But who? A few weeks ago, Charles would have been a prime candidate. But now he and Lloyd were thick as thieves, so that was out.

Then Ed had an idea. He could call one of the ministers of the larger black churches in town. There was one in particular for which the *Ledger* had sponsored a youth conference last year with some free advertising in the paper. Ed had spoken with him a few times, and the pastor seemed like a reasonable guy, one of the more responsible black leaders in Houston.

Ed couldn't remember the pastor's name, but recalled putting the pastor's business card in his desk drawer. Ed opened his drawer and rifled through the note pads, breath mint boxes, pens and pencils he had stashed there.

He pulled out the stack of about a hundred business cards that were grouped together with a rubber band, and he started going through them one by one. If he found the card, he was sure he would recognize it.

After going through about half of the cards, he found it. Bishop Jeremiah Taylor, senior pastor of the New Inspiration Tabernacle. His church was one of the largest black churches in Houston with over 15,000 members. The church had locations in both the north and south sections of town, as well as a Christian academy for pre-school through sixth grade, and a nursing home. The bishop was also founder and chairman of the Houston Black Ministers Coalition, a group that touted two hundred member churches representing about 100,000 black Houstonians.

Ed knew that a lot of the large non-profit groups exaggerated their membership numbers. But Taylor had ready access to powerful folks in Houston's political and business arenas, including the mayor, the county commissioners and even the Texas governor. Ed hoped he could get the bishop to call Lloyd and persuade him to drop the whole religious angle. He didn't want to have to take further action and get Bubba involved, but Lloyd was in way over his head.

Ed dialed the number to the church office at New Inspiration, and the church secretary answered on the first ring.

"New Inspiration Tabernacle, Bishop Taylor's office."

"This is Ed Jackson, editor of the *Houston Ledger*. Is Bishop Taylor in?"

"Oh, hello, Mr. Jackson. He's meeting with Pastor Green of Main Street Baptist Church right now. But I think they're almost done. I'll check and see," she said, as she put Ed on hold and rang the bishop's office.

"Bishop Taylor," she said, when he answered, "Mr. Jackson of the *Houston Ledger* is holding for you on line one. Would you like to take the call or would you like me to take a message?"

"Tell him to hold one moment and I'll take the call," the bishop replied.

While Ed was waiting for Taylor to answer, he thought through exactly what he would say. He had to approach this carefully. He'd had enough run-ins with black preachers to know that they tended to be extremely sensitive to any signs of disrespect from the city's white establishment. But he didn't have long to collect his thoughts before Taylor came on the line.

"Bishop Taylor here."

"Bishop Taylor, it's Ed Jackson over at the *Ledger*. How are you doing?"

"My secretary told me who it was and, I must say, this is certainly a surprise. How can I help you?"

"It's funny you would ask me that because I do need your help. I'm having a problem with one of my reporters here at the paper. It's a sensitive subject, you see, and I thought you might be able to help."

"Would this be one of your black reporters?"

"Well, yes, how did you know?"

"I didn't think you would be calling me otherwise. What's this all about?"

Ed was somewhat embarrassed, but not so much that he was willing to retreat. He knew he had to present the dilemma without appearing to be critical of Lloyd or he could blow it. "You know the reporter Lloyd Palmer, don't you?"

"The reporter who solved the Pauley kidnapping?"

"Yes, Bishop, that's him."

"I don't know him personally, but I certainly know about the outstanding work he did reporting on that case. We need a dozen more like him. He's giving you problems?"

"Well, Bishop, it's more like a misunderstanding."

"From what I've seen, his demeanor seems to be non-confrontational. Have you tried talking to him?"

"Well, Bishop, as I said, it's a sensitive subject. You see, he's written a very controversial article about some African tribe that's supposed to be related to Moses or something. I've explained to him that, without irrefutable proof, we can't move forward with the story. But he's insisting that we run it right away. All I'm asking him to do is wait until we can verify the facts."

Ed knew he was manipulating the details to suit his own purposes. But unless Bishop Taylor could reason with Lloyd, he didn't see any alternative than to involve Bubba, which he really preferred not to do.

"After being so thorough about getting the facts in the Pauley case," responded Taylor, "why would Palmer do an about face and get sloppy with his reporting all of a sudden? It doesn't add up."

The bishop did have a point, Ed thought, as he chose his next words carefully.

"I think his enthusiasm may have clouded his judgment a little. He's not being very receptive to what I have to say right now. But I thought if you called him and talked to him, he might listen to you."

There were a few seconds of silence on the phone as Ed waited for Bishop Taylor's response.

"Mr. Jackson, as I said, I don't know Palmer personally, and I'm not sure if I could be any help to you at all."

"You're a well-respected man in Houston's black community, Bishop. In the whole city, in fact. Everyone knows that, including Lloyd. All I'm asking is that you talk to him."

"If you think it will make a difference, Mr. Jackson, I'll call him and see what I can do. What's his phone number?"

Ed gave Lloyd's phone number to the bishop, then said, "I really appreciate this, Bishop. Hopefully, the *Ledger* can work with you and your congregation next year on some of your projects."

Ed wanted Taylor to know that his favor would not go unnoticed when the time came for the *Ledger* to allocate their sponsorship dollars for advertising next year. "'Bye, Pastor, and I'll be in touch," said Ed, as he hung up the phone.

CHAPTER 40

Bishop Jeremiah Taylor put his office phone back on its cradle. Jackson's implication was crystal clear: Taylor had to use his considerable influence to get Palmer to back off on his story idea. Otherwise, New Inspiration Tabernacle could forget about the *Ledger*'s advertising sponsorship for its upcoming women's conference.

One thing Taylor didn't like about being senior pastor of one of the largest churches in Houston was the necessity of building quid pro quo relationships with the political and corporate establishment. When he needed permits to add more buildings to his growing ecumenical empire, or favorable media coverage for sponsorship dollars for one of his church's numerous outreach ministries, he could count on it.

But the sponsorship dollars were only a small portion of what could be at stake. Ed Jackson often sent people to the Tabernacle who were looking for places to donate money to a worthy cause. Some of these characters obviously were involved in shady dealings and were looking for a way to launder money. They'd bring thousands of dollars in cash to the church office after hours, and Taylor would write them a check for the funds, minus a handling fee, of course.

Yet when the requests came in from the powers-that-be to return the favors, he also knew he had to play ball. Otherwise, the open doors he had been able to rely upon for the past twenty years could be abruptly closed.

Taylor had been doing God's work for most of his adult life and the fruits of his labor were visible through his opulent lifestyle. Ousted as assistant pastor from a traditional Baptist church in the late 1980s after one of the female members falsely accused him of making unwanted advances, Taylor decided to start his own church from the ground up.

New Inspiration Tabernacle was established with a corporate board, with him and his wife, Trista, as the only officers with voting power. With that type of structure, he could make decisions without the restraints, oversight and constant second-guessing of a deacon or trustee board.

The Bishop had started the Tabernacle in an office park with only a handful of members. His flock had grown steadily during the first few years, but once he built a sanctuary, the growth became rapid. He now had three services on Sunday, just enough to accommodate the present membership, and he might have to add a fourth.

A solid chunk of his members were tithers, donating ten percent of their weekly income to the church, and they also contributed substantially to the pastoral fund. Taylor and his wife lived in a lavish mansion on three acres of land;

he drove a silver Porsche Carrera GT, and she sported around Houston in a red Maybach. They both traveled to out-of-town speaking engagements in a private jet.

One of Taylor's favorite scriptures was Deuteronomy 8:18: *But you shall remember the LORD your God: for it is he that gives you power to get wealth, that he may establish his covenant which he swore to your fathers, as it is this day.*

He firmly believed that the power and influence he had been bestowed due to his position in the ministry had been ordained by God. Receiving calls from people like Ed Jackson was part of that divine assignment.

Yet, after speaking with Jackson, he was baffled. He couldn't remember the last time he'd seen or spoken with the *Ledger*'s editor, and they weren't exactly running buddies. He didn't like being dragged into what seemed to be an internal dispute at Houston's daily newspaper.

But he couldn't afford to let this Palmer fellow jeopardize his relationship with the men who ran the *Ledger* over a topic that the reporter wasn't really qualified to discuss. After all, had Palmer been trained at a seminary or did he have a degree in religious studies? Had he been called by God to decipher the holy scriptures? He ought to leave the Biblical analysis to men like Taylor who had spent years combing through the scriptures and who were anointed to interpret them.

His belief that Palmer was overstepping his boundaries, inserting himself into areas that were simply out of his league, was how Bishop Taylor justified picking up the phone and making the call. When Lloyd answered, the Bishop was ready.

"Mr. Palmer, this is Bishop Jeremiah Taylor of the New Inspiration Tabernacle. First, let me congratulate you on a job well done on solving the Pauley kidnapping crisis. I don't know what would have happened if you hadn't acted as quickly as you did."

Lloyd was on his lunch break when he received the call. He'd become accustomed to receiving these types of congratulatory phone calls for the past few weeks and didn't think it out of the ordinary.

"Why, thank you Bishop Taylor. That means a lot coming from you and the other religious leaders who have called."

"That was one of the reasons for my phone call, but I do have something else I'd like to discuss with you."

"Oh? What can I do for you, Bishop Taylor?"

Taylor paused for a few seconds; he wanted to have just the right tone in his voice. "I understand that you're working on a religious piece for the *Ledger*."

"Yes, I am. How did you know about that?"

Taylor toyed with the idea of telling Palmer that Jackson had called him, but he decided it would be best not to. "Let's just say that I hear things from time to time. I receive calls from people from all walks of life, and let's just say I heard a rumor. Can you tell me exactly what the article is about?"

Lloyd thought it strange that he was getting a call from the Bishop about a newspaper story, and he had a sneaking suspicion that Ed was the instigator behind this phone call. But he couldn't figure out what was in it for Bishop Taylor. "Well, I'd rather not go into all of the details before the article actually runs, Bishop Taylor. Someone might get wind of the idea and steal it right from under me. I've had that happen before, you know."

"Does it relate to the Bible in some way?"

"As a matter of fact, it does. The book of Exodus, to be exact." Lloyd had read more of the Bible recently and found that the book of Exodus included extensive descriptions of both Aaron and Moses, who led the Israelites out of bondage by the Egyptians.

"Since I'm assuming that you don't have a background in religious studies or a degree in theology, wouldn't it be a good idea for you to consult with one of the ordained ministers of the city, or even a group of ministers, before moving forward with your article?"

"With all due respect, Bishop Taylor, I've already done extensive research and have a first-hand source for much of the material in my article. It's really not the kind of story that would require input from members of the Houston clergy. But I appreciate the offer. Is that all you needed?" Lloyd was ready to cut this conversation short. The Bishop was evidently on a mission, one at which Lloyd would make sure he failed.

The Bishop hadn't expected the phone call to end so abruptly. "Are you sure there's nothing I or other members of the Coalition can do?"

"I'm positive, Bishop. I appreciate the call, and much success to you and the members of the Tabernacle," Lloyd said, as he hung up the phone. If that's the way Ed wanted to play it, Lloyd thought, he could make some phone calls of his own.

CHAPTER 41

The news from Bishop Taylor wasn't good. Ed thought he had better than a fifty-fifty shot at getting Lloyd to back off by having Taylor call him. At the very least, he thought there was a good chance of getting him to table the article about that African tribe so he wouldn't have to run it in the upcoming special section that was due to run in less than two weeks. Instead his plan may have backfired completely. From the feedback Ed received from Bishop Taylor, the phone call may have agitated Lloyd to the point where he'd dug in his heels.

But there was no way on God's green earth that Ed was going to run Lloyd's article. He didn't care what kind of pressure came from the rich guys upstairs or anywhere else. They weren't going to have to take the heat from the good old boys inside and outside Houston. He'd be eaten alive with phone calls from Kingwood, Magnolia, Conroe, Friendswood — suburban cities with older white populations that still actually read newspapers and didn't get all of their news from the Internet.

Nope. Ed wasn't going to let Lloyd Palmer, or any nigger at the *Houston Ledger,* tell him what he had to run in his newspaper. He would have to get Bubba involved after all. Ed didn't see any other way to handle it. He'd tried the diplomatic approach with Taylor and it had gotten him nowhere.

But he had to make sure there were six degrees of separation between him and whatever Bubba decided to do. If Bubba did his usual meticulous job, everybody — including Lloyd — would believe that what happened was purely accidental.

He dialed Bubba's number. "Bubba, this is Ed."

"Wow, two calls within the same month. This might just be a record, since I normally don't hear from you more than twice within the same year. But I was kinda of expecting you to call."

"Yeah, why is that?"

"I've been seeing your boy, Lloyd, on the T.V. That nigger is a cocky son of a bitch, isn't he? That's what happens when you give one of those coons a little status. It goes straight to their head."

Ed rolled his eyes. He agreed with Bubba, but didn't have time to rehash the past now. "I'm already aware of that, Bubba, and I can't talk long. I'm still at work. You know what we talked about at Fuddrucker's, right?"

"Yeah, you wanted me to take care of him if he got out of line. The only question is how far do you want me to go?"

"I don't want him killed or anything, because that would create too much investigation. Lloyd has almost reached celebrity status in the city and the shock to the political system would be immense. But I do want the bejesus scared out of him, enough so he'll back off and stop causing me problems. He might even be scared enough to quit, which would be fine with me. Just make sure whatever you do looks like an accident, okay?"

"Don't worry, Ed. I know just what to do. Transfer the money for this one to the usual account, and I'll get started right away."

"When do you think you'll have it done? I need to get this nigger off my back as soon as possible."

"Oh, so it's a rush job, huh. Today's Wednesday. I'll have it done before Friday morning. Is that good enough?"

"That's perfect. I guess you won't need to call me and tell me when it's done. I'll find out once the news breaks about him. It's probably best that we don't talk to each other for awhile anyway."

"Don't worry, Ed. I won't show up at your office and embarrass you. We'll keep our relationship quiet, like we always have. I swear, Ed, sometimes you make me feel like I'm your mistress or something with you not wanting to be seen with me in the daylight," Bubba said with a hearty laugh.

"It's a good thing I'm not sensitive about that kind of thing," Bubba continued. "We're from two different worlds, always have been and probably always will be.

"But it doesn't matter how far up the corporate ladder you go, you'll always be part of the old neighborhood. As long as you don't forget that, we can still be buddies."

"I won't forget, Bubba, and I'm grateful to you for saving my ass, this time and the other times too."

Ed hung up the phone and smiled to himself. Lloyd Palmer thought he had Ed over a barrel, but Ed would get the last laugh.

CHAPTER 42

Audrey Moore usually didn't work late on Wednesday nights. She enjoyed going to her mid-week Bible study meeting at her church and liked to leave by at least five thirty. But today she had some letters she had to finish writing and sending for Mr. Jackson and decided to stay until they were done.

With her purse in hand, she had walked toward his office door, which was slightly ajar, to tell him she was about to go home when she overheard him talking on the phone. He was speaking with a low volume, and it was obvious that his conversation was not for public consumption. As she approached the door she heard him say, ". . . I don't want him killed," and she stopped in her tracks. Who could he be talking about?

Audrey stood quietly by the door and continued to listen. From his conversation, it was obvious that Ed was talking to someone about having a man hurt in some way to teach him a lesson. Then she heard him mention Lloyd's name and she gasped. Could he be talking about Lloyd Palmer? He had to be since she knew that, ever since the Pauley kidnapping, there had been friction between Ed and Lloyd.

She didn't want Ed to know she was still there so, when it sounded as though his conversation was coming to an end, she quietly tiptoed backwards toward the exit. Once she got outside, she ran to her car, got in and locked the doors. Her heart was beating loudly in her chest and her hands were shaking. She had to get out of there before Mr. Jackson came out of the building, so she put the key in the ignition and gingerly wheeled away.

Audrey still couldn't believe what she heard, but she knew her ears didn't deceive her. She had to warn Lloyd, but she knew he'd never believe her. In fact, he probably wouldn't even accept her call.

Audrey had been single since she divorced her husband five years ago. She still had a voluptuous figure, with healthy double-D cups at the top, and had her fair share of dates. She was really attracted to Lloyd; even though she knew he was married, she couldn't help herself. Not only was he handsome, but he didn't treat her like a sex object as did so many others. He really seemed to respect her, both as a woman and for her considerable office skills and the pride she took in her work.

She wasn't just trying to skate by on her looks alone and had obtained her associate degree in office administration from Lone Star Community College. She had also taken a few courses in business law, just to make sure she had other options if the job with the *Ledger* disappeared.

But no matter how hard she tried, Lloyd just wouldn't respond to her advances. Gosh, his wife was really lucky to have a husband so committed to her and their family. If only Audrey's first husband hadn't been a rolling stone, spending most of his time chasing women and drinking.

She not only had to warn Lloyd, but she also had to figure out a way to expose Ed Jackson. She had worked at the *Ledger* for five years, and she didn't think the upper management would approve of his actions; if for no other reason than that the bad publicity and legal liability for the *Ledger* would be catastrophic, perhaps leading to the company's demise. There could even be class action suits from former employees who had faced discrimination.

But she didn't have any proof. It was just her word against Ed's from a phone conversation she overheard. If confronted, he would simply deny the whole thing, fire her, and even label her psychotic or delusional. Losing her job may be the least of her worries if she revealed what she knew. Her life could be in danger too.

During her drive home, she mulled over her options. She had to do something now. It sounded as though the threat to Lloyd was imminent and could occur within the next couple of days.

When she arrived at her apartment building and pulled into her assigned parking space, she turned off the ignition, sat for a few minutes and thought about who she could call. Then she had an "aha moment." She would call Charles Scott.

CHAPTER 43

Bubba Murray was sitting in his den with his feet perched atop the coffee table and a can of Colt 45 malt liquor in hand, relaxing, as he prepared his mind for the job he would do later that night. Ed was such a weakling, Bubba thought, afraid to stand up to niggers and anyone else who got in his way. With him, it was all about his precious status as editor of the *Ledger*. He'd do just about anything to protect that.

Bubba's daddy had taught him that the best way to handle niggers was by force and intimidation. Isolate one of 'em and threaten 'em within an inch of his life. All they needed was to see an example made of a fellow soul brother, and the rest of them would fold like a house of cards.

That's what they'd done a few years back when a nigger family moved into the old neighborhood. Bubba and his friends started by throwing a brick through the front window. When that didn't work, they killed the family's cat and left the carcass on the front porch with its throat slit. The family finally got the message, packed their bags and moved out. The word got around, and no more niggers had tried to move in since then.

It had been a while since he'd received an assignment from Ed. Ed only called as a last resort, when the niggers at the paper got out of line and Ed's intimidation tactics didn't work.

The last time was about three years ago when Ed had the hots for a black woman who worked at the *Ledger*. Ed started sending her anonymous notes at first, letting her know she had a secret admirer at the office. He thought she would recognize his handwriting and respond to his advances.

After that, he was anticipating some changes in her behavior towards him, but nothing happened. One day at the office, Ed grabbed her ass, and she threatened to file a sexual harassment suit. The head honchos at the paper didn't tolerate actions by management that could get the paper in legal hot water. If the guys upstairs got wind of it, Ed would have lost his job and most of his pension; plus he'd be blackballed in the industry.

But Bubba had taken care of that. He parked outside her house one night and waited until she left. He went inside, located the gas line in the kitchen pantry, and severed it with a pipe cutter. When she got home and turned on the light switch—BOOM —the house exploded. She survived, but she had second and third degree burns on her entire body. She spent months in rehab and would be collecting disability checks for years to come.

Ed was happy because his problem was solved. No more sexual harassment suit, and no fingers pointing at him.

But the niggers had gotten really uppity since the election of that Muslim from Illinois—Obama. Bubba still wasn't convinced Obama was born in the good ole USA.

Some of his pals at the lodge told him about a tape of Obama's grandmother admitting that she was present at his birth in Kenya. The liberal media had taken care of that, suppressed the tape and paid off the guy's grandma.

Since Obama had been in the White House, some of these niggers had gotten the idea in their heads that they were actually running things. Bubba was certain that's what happened with this Lloyd Palmer fellow. His situation was a bit more complicated than the sexual harassment dust-up, but nothing Bubba couldn't handle. He'd thought of a way to get that nigger reporter out of the picture, for good.

Ed didn't want Palmer killed, but sometimes the misadventures Bubba planned for his targets spiraled out of control, Bubba thought, as he smiled to himself. He couldn't be responsible if Palmer met with an untimely death, now could he? He had the perfect scheme, and everyone, even the law enforcement officers, would think it was just an accident.

He would cut the front and rear brake lines on Palmer's car later tonight. Houston was a city with relatively flat terrain, except on freeway ramps. Palmer had to take the freeway to go to work every day, and getting on and off Houston's freeways would require that he go up steep inclines and onto downhill ramps.

Bubba had already cased Palmer's house and vehicle. Once he'd met with Ed at Fuddrucker's a few weeks ago, he figured he'd eventually get the call. That was how Ed usually handled things. If Ed told Bubba he had a problem that might need fixin', he'd always call him within a few days with the go ahead.

Palmer parked his car on the street in front of his house. His wife parked her car in the driveway or the garage. Once Palmer left home for the office, or to any destination, his brakes would fail. Depending on how fast he was going, he wouldn't be able to stop and would experience a head-on collision with another vehicle or a cement barrier.

Palmer's vehicle might even careen over the side of the ramp, crash onto the cement pavement below, and burst into flames. Then there would be very little evidence for the cops to examine. There could be some collateral damage, but when it came to keeping the niggers in line, Bubba's attitude was that sometimes a few people had to be sacrificed for the greater good.

Bubba gulped down the last of his beer, belched, leaned back in his lounge chair, and picked up the T.V. remote control. He kept channel surfing until he landed on a professional basketball game and began watching it.

Those coons ought to just stick to sports and entertainment where they belonged, Bubba thought. If they'd just stay in their place, he wouldn't have to take these kinds of actions. If only they'd stay in their place.

CHAPTER 44

Audrey had Charles' cell phone number because she sometimes had to contact the reporters after normal working hours. She had thought about what she was going to say to him and thought it would be best to just get to the point quickly. She was hoping he would believe her and would tell her what to do. Audrey was clueless, and frightened.

Ed wasn't the most sociable guy at the *Ledger*, especially where the black employees were concerned. But Audrey never imagined he would be capable of something like this. She'd seen this sort of thing happen in the movies and on the news, but she thought the kind of extreme measures Ed was discussing on the phone were relics of the past. Yet, the Pauley kidnapping had given her a dose of reality.

Mrs. Pauley joined a long line of other criminals who had committed heinous acts and pointed the finger at black men: Susan Smith of South Carolina, who drowned her two sons in a lake, then claimed she was carjacked by a black man who stole her car and her children.

Bonnie Sweeten of Pennsylvania, who claimed she was abducted by two black men and, a few days later, was found in Disney World with her daughter. Charles Stuart, a Massachusetts man who shot himself and killed his pregnant wife for the insurance money, then blamed it on a black man.

Audrey's hands shook as she selected Charles from among her contacts and pressed *send*. When he answered, she heard loud music and voices in the background. It sounded like he was either at a party or the bar that was one of Charles' regular hangouts.

"Hello, Charles?"

"Yeah, you've got him. Who's this?" Charles said, putting his finger in his right ear in an attempt to hear the caller.

"Charles, this is Audrey from the office. I really need to talk to you. Can you hear me?"

"Audrey? From the office? Wow, I can't remember the last time you called. Let me go outside so I can hear better," Charles said, as he walked toward the entrance to the bar he had gone to for happy hour. Once he got outside, he gave the phone call his full attention.

"What's up, Audrey? It must be something important for you to call me."

"Charles, I'm really scared and I need your help."

Charles was puzzled. He'd had very few one-on-one conversations with Audrey, and they certainly weren't close friends. "What happened, Audrey? Talk to me."

"Lloyd's in danger, Charles. And I could be in danger, too, if anyone finds out."

Now Charles was beginning to understand. He knew Audrey had a thing for Lloyd, but he didn't think she'd take it this far, and he didn't want to do anything to encourage her. "Audrey, what is this all about? If you're trying to use me to get close to Lloyd, it won't work. He's already told you he's happily married."

"This isn't about me trying to hook up with Lloyd, Charles. Ed set some sort of plan in motion for Lloyd to be hurt. I would call Lloyd myself, but he'd never believe me. But if you call him, he'll take it seriously."

"Ed? Are you talking about Ed Jackson, our boss?"

"You're damned right I'm talking about Ed Jackson. I was working late at the office, and I overheard him talking on the phone to somebody.

"I'm not sure who it was, but I distinctly heard him say that he didn't want Lloyd killed. He just wanted to scare him so he would back off."

"I left the office in a hurry," continued Audrey, "quietly, but in a hurry — before Ed knew I was still there. Oh, my God, Charles, what are we going to do?"

"Are you sure you heard it right, Audrey? Maybe you misunderstood."

"Charles, how could I misunderstand a thing like that? Ed mentioned Lloyd by name. He wasn't talking about something he saw on television. He was giving whoever was on the other end of the phone instructions on how to handle things, and he said to make sure it looked like an accident.

"He also said that he wanted whatever was planned to happen soon. Charles, we've got to do something."

Charles still couldn't believe what he was hearing. He knew that Ed and Lloyd's relationship had deteriorated ever since the Pauley kidnapping, but was Ed capable of violence? Would he take his anger to the level of potentially hiring a contract killer or a muscle man? Charles had worked at the *Ledger* for more than five years and he hadn't seen that side of Ed.

But Audrey was clearly disturbed; in fact, he'd never known her to be so agitated about anything. Around the office, she was all smiles and rarely seemed rattled. With all of the pressure the reporters and staff experienced as news deadlines approached, Audrey could always be depended upon to be as cool as a cucumber.

"Okay, Audrey. If I assume you're telling me the truth, then I have to think about what to do next. We need to warn Lloyd, but you have to give me something credible so he'll believe us.

"I hate to say this, but it would probably have been best if it had been anybody except you who overheard the conversation. Lloyd is going to be very skeptical, and I can't blame him."

"Believe me, I wish somebody else had overheard it too. Right now, I'm afraid for Lloyd and for me too. Charles, I'm afraid to go home. What if Ed finds out I was working late today? What if he heard me when I left the office? What if he saw me driving away from the building?" Audrey was hyperventilating.

"Okay, Audrey. Don't panic. That's more what-ifs than we could possibly answer right now. Let me think for a second."

Charles contemplated Audrey's dilemma. The first thing he had to do was make sure she was safe. "Do you have a friend you can spend the night with tonight until we can get this all sorted out?"

"I can call my girlfriend, Tangela, and she'll let me stay at her house. But I really don't want to get anyone else involved in this. Should I tell her what's going on?"

"Absolutely not. That would be too dangerous. Just make up a story—something like there's a problem with your air conditioner or your water pressure's not working, and you can't take a shower. This is just a precaution anyway, since you don't think Ed knows you overheard his phone call. That way, you will at least feel safe until tomorrow."

Charles paused, thinking about how Audrey might react to seeing Ed at work the next day. "And maybe you should call in sick in the morning, just to be on the safe side. There's no way you would be able to act normal around Ed after this, and if you are nervous or acting weird, he might get suspicious."

"Okay, but Charles, what are you going to do?"

"I'm not sure yet. I have to warn Lloyd, but I have to think of the best approach. Be sure to keep your cell phone handy, and I'll either call you or text you."

Audrey sensed that Charles was apprehensive, and she wanted something done right away. She couldn't put her life on hold, and, as far as she was concerned, Ed Jackson should be in jail. "When will I hear from you, Charles? How long will I have to wait?"

"It shouldn't be long. I need to talk to Lloyd, but I want to meet with him face to face. I don't know if dropping by his house unannounced is a good idea, and I don't want to go into too much detail over the phone. After all, if what you say is true, his house and his phone lines may be monitored."

"I hadn't thought of that," said Audrey, "so I guess I'll wait to hear from you. Do you want my friend's address?"

"Not for now. It's probably better that no one knows where you are, including me. I'll call you as soon as I can."

"Thanks for handling this, Charles. I don't know what I would have done if I hadn't been able to reach you. Bye."

Audrey ended the phone call, then went to her apartment so she could pack an overnight bag. It was going to be a long night.

CHAPTER 45

Charles was pacing back and forth on the sidewalk in front of the bar where he'd been when Audrey called. He knew he had to contact Lloyd tonight. If Audrey was right, there was little time to spare. Ed's accomplice might have already set his plan in motion.

Charles wished Audrey had more details so he would know what to tell Lloyd to expect. But, based on Audrey's account, Ed seemed to prefer to be kept in the dark about the sinister plot. Then he'd have what politicians, mobsters and lawyers called "plausible deniability." Even under interrogation, Ed wouldn't be able to help the authorities, except to reveal the identity of his accomplice. And the chances he would do so were virtually nil since he wouldn't risk incriminating himself in the process.

The first priority was to inform Lloyd without alarming his wife, Stephanie. It was already after nine o'clock, and Charles knew Lloyd usually went to bed at about eleven. He decided to text Lloyd in hopes that his cell phone was nearby.

I need you to meet me at Charlie's Bar in Jersey Village in thirty minutes. Very important.

Charles sent the text and hoped for a quick response. He was in the throes of putting together a Plan B, in case Lloyd didn't answer, when a reply came back.

It's late. Can't it wait until tomorrow morning?

Charles pecked out: *No it can't. I need you to meet me NOW. A matter of life and death, but keep it between us. Don't tell Stephanie.* He was pretty sure the message would get Lloyd out the door and into his car.

OMG. Okay. I'm on my way.

Tense, nervous, confounded. Charles was experiencing all of these emotions and more. It would take Lloyd about twenty minutes to get there if he left right after he got the text message. Charles decided to go inside and get another drink to calm his nerves. The buzz he had before Audrey called had worn off completely.

He sat at the bar and ordered a scotch on the rocks, which he gulped down quickly, and ordered another. He'd better slow down, he thought. If he was visibly inebriated when Lloyd arrived, then he'd never be able to convince him that this was real.

Charles could hardly believe it himself. His profession as a reporter had taught him to be skeptical. Yet his gut reaction was that Audrey was telling the truth. Apparently, Ed felt sufficiently threatened by Lloyd's elevated stature that he was willing to go to great lengths to silence him. Incredible, simply incredible.

The first thing Charles had to do was convince Lloyd the threat was real. This would be no small feat with Audrey involved.

Then they'd have to figure out what he could do for protection, which wouldn't be easy either since they had no idea of the nature of the threat. It could come from anywhere.

After that they would need proof of Ed's involvement, proof which really didn't exist. Their only proof would be uncovered if there was an attempt on Lloyd's life or some sort of freak accident happened. Which meant Lloyd might have to serve himself up as bait.

A man like Ed Jackson could no longer be allowed to run a first-class operation like the *Houston Ledger*. Charles would do everything he could to make sure Ed went to jail — the sooner, the better.

CHAPTER 46

Charles kept his eyes focused on the bar's front door so he could see Lloyd the minute he walked in. He continued to nurse his scotch on the rocks, gulping some down, circling his index finger along the top rim of the glass, then picking up the glass and swirling around its contents. He finally drained his glass and decided to order just one more.

Just as the bartender placed his refill on the bar counter, Lloyd arrived. Charles waved him over to the bar, and Lloyd walked over and sat down on the barstool beside him.

Lloyd had a look of utter frustration on his face. "This had better be good. Stephanie wasn't too happy about me going out to a bar on a weeknight. Since you didn't want me to tell her about the situation, I just said I was meeting you here because we had something to talk about. She didn't say anything, but the vibe she was putting out said it all."

Charles took another gulp of scotch. He needed some liquid courage. "Lloyd, I don't know exactly how to break this to you, but I'm pretty sure you're in some sort of danger. You may need to leave town for a few days."

"Whoa . . . wait a minute. What are you talking about? Charles, how many drinks have you had since you've been sitting here?"

"I'm dead serious, Lloyd. I've had a couple of drinks, but I'm not drunk. As a matter of fact, I could use a couple more," said Charles, as he motioned to the bartender.

"You need to be more specific, Charles. Exactly what kind of danger?"

Charles swallowed hard. "I think Ed hired someone to hurt you, to scare you off."

Lloyd's expression went from surprise to puzzlement. "That's pretty farfetched, Charles. Ed's a racist son of a bitch, but do you think he'd take things that far? Where did you hear this?"

"I was afraid you were going to ask me that."

"Of course, I'm going to ask. How do you know your information is credible?"

"That's just it. I'm not one hundred percent certain. But I'm sure enough that I think you might need to leave town for a few days."

"Leave town? Are you going to tell me where you got your information or not?"

Charles hesitated, knowing that what he was about to say wouldn't be well received. "Audrey told me."

"Audrey? Audrey from the office?"

Lloyd stood up and faced Charles. "You've got to be kidding. I can't believe you made me drive all this way because of some antics Audrey pulled. I'm going home, Charles," Lloyd said, and he turned and walked toward the exit.

"Wait, Lloyd. This is important and I don't want to have to raise my voice for everybody in this bar to hear about it. So come back so I can explain."

Reluctantly, Lloyd walked back to the bar, unconvinced of the veracity of Charles' claim.

"This threat is real. I didn't want to believe it myself, but the more I think about it, the more convinced I become. Audrey overheard Ed on the phone."

"When did this supposedly happen?"

"She worked late today, and Ed didn't realize she was still at the office. She was about to tell him she was leaving for the evening when she overheard him say your name to someone on the phone. She also heard him say he didn't want you to be killed, just scared enough to back off."

"How do you know she's not making the whole thing up, Charles? You know what lengths Audrey has gone to trying to get me to hook up with her at work. She's tried everything short of following me into the men's room at work. This is probably a new tactic of hers to get me to notice her."

"That was my first thought too. But she really doesn't know about everything that has transpired between you and Ed since the Pauley kidnapping, so she wouldn't have any basis for believing that Ed would do you harm."

"She's scared out of her wits to the point that she's afraid to go home. In fact, she's sleeping at a friend's house tonight, and I told her not to come in to work tomorrow. I don't think she could fake that level of fear."

Upon reflection, Lloyd preferred to err on the side of caution and talk to Audrey himself.

"Get Audrey on the phone. I want to hear it from her own lips to see if this is a hoax or the real thing."

"Okay, her number is in my phone. It was the last incoming call," Charles said, as he unlocked his cell phone and hit the send button.

CHAPTER 47

After Audrey hung up the phone with Charles, she went to her apartment and packed an overnight bag with a few essential items. She then left her apartment building and headed to Southwest Houston to her best friend Tangela's house. She'd already called and asked if she could spend the night, and Tangela agreed. It wasn't unusual for her to sleep over since they had been best friends for years. Tangela wouldn't ask any questions and wouldn't pressure Audrey to talk until she was ready.

Audrey arrived at Tangela's house about nine thirty and was greeted with a hug. The two had been friends since high school, and Audrey could sense that Tangela knew something was amiss. But she didn't pry. Besides, Tangela was a registered nurse and she had to be at work by 7:00 a.m., so she was normally in bed by nine.

After showing Audrey to the guest room, giving her fresh linen and a goodnight hug, Tangela was off to bed. Audrey, however, doubted if she would get much sleep that night. She had never been more frightened about anything in her life.

Once she dressed for bed, she decided to try reading a novel she'd started in hopes she could relax. She expected a call from Charles some time later and had her cell phone on the night stand.

She didn't have to wait long. Her phone rang shortly after ten. She checked the display and the call was from Charles.

"Hi, Charles. Did you talk to Lloyd yet?"

"This is Lloyd, Audrey."

Audrey was taken aback. She hadn't expected to speak with Lloyd directly and thought Charles would be the intermediary between them.

"Hi, Lloyd. Did Charles tell you what happened?"

"He did, but why don't you tell me yourself."

"Well, like I told Charles, I was on my way out of the office when I overheard Ed on the phone. He was talking about you, Lloyd, and he was instructing someone to hurt you and make it look like an accident."

"What were his exact words, Audrey?"

"I can't remember every single word he said, but the part I can't forget, that I keep playing over and over in my mind, was that he said he didn't want you to be killed. He just wanted you to be scared — scared enough to quit."

"Audrey, are you absolutely sure about this? Are you sure you're not exaggerating just a little bit?"

"Lloyd, as God as my witness, I'm telling you the truth. Do you think I would make up something like this? I know I may have come on a little too strong in the past, but I would never lie about something this dangerous."

Lloyd was starting to believe Audrey's account although he still found it hard to fathom that Ed would take things so far.

"Do you have any idea who Ed was talking to?"

"No. He never said the name of the person on the other end, so I don't have any idea who it might be. But it had to have been someone he trusted to do his dirty work and keep quiet about it. Lloyd, I'm scared. What if Ed finds out I know something, and he sends the guy after me? I might have to quit my job and leave town."

"Audrey, let's not be hasty. We have to think this through. I do appreciate you telling me this and I want to make sure you're safe. Where are you now?"

"I'm at my girlfriend's house."

"Can you stay there for a day or two while Charles and I figure out what to do?"

"Okay, my friend won't mind. But I can't hide out here forever. I've got some sick days I can take, but I'll have to let them know something at the *Ledger*. I just can't go back there as long as Ed is there."

"Charles told me he recommended you call in sick tomorrow, and I think that's good advice. Just lay low until you hear from us, okay?"

Audrey felt better knowing that Lloyd and Charles were now involved. "You two be careful, okay? After overhearing Ed, who knows what he's capable of."

"Thanks, Audrey, and I really do appreciate you telling me this. Either Charles or I will give you a call tomorrow to check on you. Bye."

Lloyd hung up, took a deep breath and looked at Charles. "Well, Audrey sounds legit," he said, as he shook his head and then pounded his fist on the bar counter. "When I get my hands on Ed, I'm going to knock the crap out of him."

"I agree that Ed should be dealt with, but you've got a bigger problem," Charles replied. "He's already given the go-ahead to whomever he's hired, and we don't know what to expect or when to expect it."

"Whoa, you're right," Lloyd said, and then he had a horrible thought. "Oh my God, I've got to get Stephanie and Bria out of the house. Their lives might be in danger."

Lloyd shuddered at the thought of harm coming to either his wife or his daughter. He became consumed with making sure they were safe.

"Let's go," said Charles, shattering the temporary silence that had engulfed them. "I'll ride with you in case something goes down."

CHAPTER 48

Few words passed between Lloyd and Charles during the ride to Lloyd's house. They were both attempting to digest the gravity of the evening's events and come to grips with the new reality: The editor of the *Houston Ledger* had hired a muscle man to hurt Lloyd. For all they knew, he could even be an assassin.

Lloyd reflected on the last text message he received from Hamisi: *Watch, fight and pray.* At the time that he read it, he dismissed it as just another one of Hamisi's many riddles. But he should know by now that Hamisi was anything but frivolous. His pronouncements were always a harbinger of things to come.

Lloyd was the first to break the silence. "Thanks for making sure I knew what was going on and for riding with me, Charles. It really means a lot. You could have just dismissed Audrey's accusations, and then God only knows what might have happened."

"No thanks is necessary, Lloyd. I'm sure if our situations were reversed, you'd do the same for me."

Charles reached inside his jacket and pulled a revolver from his belt. "By the way, I have my gun with me."

Charles had retrieved it from his car's glove compartment before they left the bar. "I keep it in my car for protection. We might need it, and better safe than sorry."

"Do you know how to use that thing?" asked Lloyd.

"Don't worry. I've had lots of practice at the firing range. The last thing we want is to be featured in the *Ledger* for shooting at the assailant -- and missing."

They both laughed. It was a nervous kind of laughter, meant to relieve the tension they both felt. In the state of Texas, anyone who wasn't a convicted felon was allowed to purchase and carry a firearm. And defending one's home was considered sacrosanct. An intruder into someone's home in Texas could be shot by the home owner without question.

Lloyd had decided not to call Stephanie while they were in route. He wanted to help get her and Bria ready to leave and would only divulge what was absolutely necessary for now. She would instinctively know something was terribly wrong, but she would do what he asked. He had already called Ron to let him know what was happening, and Ron had agreed it would be best for Stephanie and Bria to stay with him and Shirley until the whole thing blew over.

When they arrived at Lloyd's house, he parked the car and took the key out of the ignition. But he didn't immediately exit the car. He sat for a moment, collecting his thoughts.

"Are you okay?" asked Charles, who was experiencing an adrenaline rush and was anxious to get out of the car.

"Yeah, I'm good. Let's go," replied Lloyd, as he opened the car door and headed toward the house. It was after eleven and a school night, and he knew Stephanie and Bria would probably be asleep. He'd have to wake Stephanie up and give her enough details to get her packed and out of the house, which wouldn't be easy. Since Ed's call had occurred just a few hours ago, Lloyd didn't think he was in any immediate danger. But he didn't want to take any chances.

Once they got inside, Lloyd told Charles to wait in the living room while he went upstairs. Stephanie was sleeping soundly on her stomach, and he sat by the bedside for a few seconds, then kissed her on the cheek and whispered into her left ear.

"Hon, wake up."

Stephanie stirred. "Hey, you're back huh. What did Charles want?"

"Steph, you and Bria need to get up, pack a few things and go over to Ron and Shirley's."

Stephanie had been groggy, but was wide awake now. She sat up in bed. "Why? What's going on, Lloyd?"

"I can't explain it all in detail, but Ed may have set something in motion, and I'd rather be safe than sorry. It's just an extra precaution," said Lloyd, not wanting to alarm Stephanie any more than was absolutely necessary.

"Something may go down, and I just want to make sure you and Bria are both safe." Lloyd patted Stephanie affectionately on her behind. "Hurry up. Ron and Shirley are expecting you."

Stephanie wanted more information. She knew there had to be more to what was going on than what Lloyd was willing to say. She could see it in his eyes. But she had been married to Lloyd long enough to trust his judgment. If he was responding with this much urgency, it had to be for a good reason. Once Lloyd stood up, she threw back the covers, put on her slippers and stood up beside him. She gave him a warm embrace and kissed him gently.

"Okay, Lloyd. Bria and I will be ready in fifteen minutes."

CHAPTER 49

Once Stephanie and Bria were gone, Lloyd and Charles settled in the living room where they planned to sleep for the night. If some perpetrator was going to try to get into the house, Lloyd wanted to be alert and ready.

Even if he went upstairs to their bedroom, it was doubtful he would get much sleep. Better to catch the bastard off guard, should he try something tonight. He was positioned in the lounge chair facing the front of the house and had adjusted the lever to the reclined position.

Charles had his gun with him just in case. He placed it underneath the pillow on the couch where he planned to sleep. If an intruder entered, Charles would have the pistol handy; but the guy would never know what hit him. Charles had adopted the rules from *The Art of War*, and the element of surprise was always an effective tool in any battle.

Charles was finally starting to understand what, before now, he had assumed was Lloyd's paranoia. In his wildest dreams, he would never have thought that Ed Jackson would go to such lengths for something as simple as a difference in perspective.

In his profession, Charles had always pushed the envelope a bit; that was the best way to get noticed and get ahead. Journalists were usually rewarded for thinking outside the box and using story angles that others had ignored, overlooked or never imagined.

But it seemed that all of Lloyd's attempts to do essentially the same thing resulted in resistance and outrage from Ed. Charles decided that now was the best time to share his thoughts with Lloyd.

"I want to apologize to you, Lloyd."

"Apologize? For what?"

"For doubting you, and for saying you were paranoid."

Lloyd leaned back and laid his head on the lounge chair's headrest. "From your point of view, Charles, I know the things I was trying to tell you were incredible. We're all captive of our own personal universes—our own personal experiences. You could no more understand what it's like to be a black man in America than I could imagine being in your shoes."

"Too many people buy into the notion that if something is not happening to *them*, it's not happening at all. They act as though the people who describe instances of bias and a rush to judgment have runaway imaginations."

"The fact is, Charles, that these experiences are very real. That's what happened in the case of Trayvon Martin. The guy who saw Trayvon walking down the street wearing a hoodie automatically assumed the boy was 'suspicious.' The end result was a dead teenager, whose life was senselessly cut short."

"When these situations arise, I've just learned to cope with them as best I can and still maintain some sense of self-worth. It's not easy, but I learned a long time ago that crying about things I cannot change is a complete waste of time. But, Charles, I appreciate the fact that you stuck with me, in spite of your doubts."

Lloyd was seated, but he stood up and offered Charles his right hand for a handshake. Instead, Charles stood up and gave him a man hug.

"How do you think Ed's accomplice — whoever he is — will come at you?" asked Charles.

"Your guess is as good as mine. But didn't Audrey say that Ed wanted it to look like an accident?"

"Yep. That's what she said."

"Well, in that case, it's probably going to be pretty subtle, something that is done quietly. It won't be a gunshot or a bombing because then it would be obvious that there was foul play. It's most likely going to be something we won't suspect."

"You're probably right, Lloyd," replied Charles. Then he paused, as if waiting for Lloyd to say more, but there was silence.

"What do we do about Ed? Do we call the cops?"

"Let's wait and see if anything happens tonight. We don't have any proof right now, and if we go to the police, Ed will just deny everything. Then we may be worse off than we are now. Ed will be alerted to the fact that we're on to him. And his henchman will simply crawl back into his hole and wait for another time to strike. Then where will we be?"

"Let's just wait and see what happens," repeated Lloyd. "But I'm going to be sleeping with one eye open."

Lloyd went over to the lamp adjacent to the couch and turned off the light. "Let's try to get some sleep. I'm sure we'll have a long day tomorrow."

He sat down and leaned back in the lounge chair, hoping nothing would happen that night but prepared for the worst. Lloyd closed his eyes, then remembered Hamisi's message: Watch, fight and *pray*. He mouthed a silent prayer for Stephanie and Bria and drifted off to sleep.

CHAPTER 50

Bubba parked his light truck about a block from the Palmer home, in an area that was not directly under any street lights. His truck was positioned so he could see the front of the house. Lloyd's car was parked out front, as it had been on the nights when Bubba had cased their home. Like so many human beings—Bubba's targets included— Lloyd was a creature of habit. They didn't know how often those habits could be used against them, Bubba thought, with a silent smirk.

He'd sit and wait until all of the lights were off before he would make his move. It was just after midnight, and a few lights were still on downstairs. The Palmers were up later than usual, Bubba noticed, but he didn't think there was any reason for concern. They would be asleep soon enough, and he could get the job done and go home. It was only going to take about five minutes to sever those brake lines, and the Palmers would never know that he'd been there.

He sat in his truck smoking a cigarette and turned on the radio to one of his favorite country stations. "Love's Gonna Make It Alright" by George Strait was playing and Bubba hummed along. It didn't get any better than George Strait when it came to country music. Bubba leaned back and relaxed.

After about thirty minutes, the downstairs lights went off in the Palmer home. Bubba checked his watch; it was 1:00 a.m. He waited a few more minutes, then looked around carefully to make sure none of the Palmers' neighbors were stirring. Everything was nice and quiet. Bubba grabbed his tool belt and got out of the truck.

He quickly strode the one block to the front of the Palmer home where Lloyd's Toyota Camry was parked. He sat down on the pavement, lay down, and scooted underneath the car. He took his flashlight and pipe cutter off his tool belt and turned the flashlight on so he could easily locate the brake line. He heard the sound of grass rustling nearby and assumed it was a cat scampering to safety. Bubba continued his work, found the brake line, and prepared to make a clean cut.

A split second later Bubba felt a pair of gloved hands on the sides of his face, but not for long. His neck was quickly snapped. Bubba was dead.

CHAPTER 51

The rays of the morning sunrise emanating through the living room window awakened Lloyd from his fitful lounge chair slumber. He checked his cell phone for the time, which was 6:30 a.m. He wanted to call Stephanie and check on her and Bria, but he decided to wait until later since she would be getting ready for work. He got up and nudged Charles to awaken him.

"Charles, wake up."

Charles opened his eyes and sat upright on the couch where he had been sleeping. "Did anything happen?"

"No. It was quiet all night. I did fall asleep, but it was never a deep sleep. I didn't hear anything all night. I'm going to make some coffee. Do you want some?"

"Sure. Are you going to make me breakfast too?" Charles joked.

"You really wouldn't want to eat my cooking. Stephanie is so good at it that I just enjoy hers. I try to stay in my lane—no need to upset the apple cart.

"But I'm sure she left something in the 'fridge that we can eat. There's some fresh fruit in the kitchen too. I put some towels in the bathroom downstairs for you, so you can wash up in there."

Lloyd went upstairs to the bathroom to wash up and brush his teeth. He decided to take a shower later on, once they decided what they were going to do.

He looked at his reflection in the mirror, and it was the same as it had been a few weeks ago when he was doing some soul searching about his career. But he was not the same Lloyd Palmer that he was before. That Lloyd Palmer no longer existed.

He went downstairs to the kitchen and looked in the refrigerator to see what would be easy to prepare, yet filling. He found a carton of eggs and decided to scramble some eggs. He and Charles could also eat some yogurt mixed with fruit and drink their coffee while they discussed their strategy for the day.

Not long after he had started scrambling the eggs, Charles emerged from the bathroom looking contemplative, but refreshed.

"Those eggs smell pretty good and I didn't realize I'd be so hungry. I guess this adrenaline rush I've had since last night burns calories because I feel like I haven't eaten in a week."

"I'm still on edge because I have no idea what's going to happen today. I'm just glad that Stephanie and Bria are in a safe place so I can concentrate on what to do. Charles, I think we need to go to the police."

"With what, Lloyd? We don't have any proof. It's just our word against Ed's, and we'll look like total idiots once Ed denies everything, which I know he will."

"Well, I figure my reputation should count for something. We'll just have to go into the nearest police station and then keep going up the chain of command until we can get someone to listen to us."

"I questioned your judgment before, and you've been right all the way so far; so I'm with you. This is definitely new for you. The old Lloyd was reluctant to ruffle the boss's feathers. Now, you're ruffling the feathers and the whole bird," laughed Charles. "But I like it. You've shown me a few things, too."

"Yeah, like what?"

"I've been pretty nonchalant about taking life too seriously. I spend most of my weekends drinking and chasing women. But there are some issues of conscience and justice that are still palpable and present. I ignored them in the past, but not anymore."

"Are you saying that your days of drinking and chasing women are over?"

"Are you kidding? Hell, no." They both laughed.

"But I'll be looking at life a little differently from now on," said Charles. "Let's eat."

After they ate, Lloyd decided to call Stephanie to let her know he was okay; that nothing had happened thus far. After both of them showered and got dressed it was about eight o'clock. They wanted to get an early start with the police since they didn't know how much convincing Lloyd would have to do and how long it would take.

Lloyd opened the front door, and Charles walked out ahead of him. Just as Lloyd was about to lock the door, Charles noticed something sticking out from underneath the car and said, "Lloyd, there's something underneath your car. It looks like a man's foot."

They cautiously descended the front steps and slowly approached the car, all the while fixated on the scuffed cowboy boot that was sticking out slightly on the passenger side near the rear of Lloyd's Camry. Charles broke the silence that engulfed them, "The foot doesn't appear to be moving," he said, then moved closer and gave the foot a slight kick.

"He's either unconscious or dead. Lloyd, this is probably the guy who was supposed to scare you off. I wonder what happened to him."

"Maybe the son of a bitch had a heart attack. Let's go back inside and call the police. This is one crime scene that I don't want disturbed since this is probably the proof we need to put Ed behind bars where he belongs."

CHAPTER 52

It only took about ten minutes for two police cars to arrive at Lloyd's house. When Lloyd called 911, he identified himself as a reporter for the *Ledger*, and that seemed to have had the desired effect. Lloyd and Charles had been waiting inside but had been looking through the front window that faced the street so they could go outside as soon as the police arrived.

Before removing the body from underneath the car, the police peppered Lloyd with questions: What time did he get home last night? What time did he notice the body? Did he hear any commotion or noises outside during the night? Did either of them touch the body? Did he know of anyone who might want to harm him?

Lloyd answered truthfully to all of the questions except the last one. He replied "I'm not sure," to the policeman who questioned him, but he knew exactly who wanted to do him harm: Ed Jackson. He wanted to find out the identity of the man who was underneath his car before he said anything.

One of the policemen spoke into his radio requesting that a van from the coroner's office be dispatched to the Lloyd residence. Then two of the cops pulled Bubba's body from underneath Lloyd's Camry.

Bubba's eyes were wide open, with a look that implied his death had been both sudden and shocking. His head dangled easily from side to side when he was moved.

"From the looks of it, I'd say his neck was broke," said one of the cops, "but I have no idea how it could have happened underneath this car." The officer turned Bubba's body over onto its stomach and checked his back for blood pooling and rigor mortis.

"Well, it's clear his body hasn't been moved based on the pooling of the blood in his back," the officer said, pointing to the area on Bubba's back where the blood had accumulated. "He died underneath this car, but I'd be hard pressed to tell you how it happened," the officer added, scratching his head with the fingers of his right hand.

"Let's check his pockets for a wallet and identification."

The officers checked Bubba's pockets, found his wallet and looked at his driver's license. "Robert Murray is the name on this license. Do either of you fellows know this guy?" said the officer, directing his question to Lloyd and Charles.

As soon as they pulled Bubba's body from underneath the car, Lloyd and Charles looked at his face to see if they recognized him, but neither of them had ever seen him before. They shook their heads.

"We've never seen him before," said Lloyd, "but I'm fairly certain who put him up to this."

"If you do know who's behind this, we can go question him right away. Who is it?"

"My boss at the *Houston Ledger*, Ed Jackson."

"Ed Jackson? Why in the world would he want to get somebody to disable your car?"

"It's a long story, officer, but, believe me, it's for real. An employee at the paper overheard Mr. Jackson on the phone yesterday evening arranging for someone to hurt me. Apparently, this guy was sent to do Ed's dirty work."

"Who overheard this phone call, and when did it supposedly occur?"

"I'd rather not say, sir, because she's in fear for her life. But it took place yesterday evening, around six o'clock."

"Well, we can't accuse Mr. Jackson of conspiracy to commit murder or attempted murder without some proof. Let me have our detectives pull Mr. Jackson's phone records at his office. If there's a connection between Mr. Murray and your editor, we'll find it. Then we'll bring him in for questioning."

CHAPTER 53

It only took the detectives a few hours to pull Ed Jackson's phone records, and, sure enough, he had spoken to Bubba several times over the course of the last month. The phone call the evening before, however, was considered to be probable cause for Ed to be brought in for questioning. They also searched Bubba's home and found his handwritten notes where he'd tracked Lloyd's comings and goings for the past couple of weeks. By late afternoon, Ed was charged with conspiracy to commit murder.

Meanwhile, Lloyd had called Stephanie to assure her that everything was okay, that the person who'd put them in harm's way was dead, and that Ed Jackson was behind bars. He also called Audrey to thank her for warning him in advance. If she hadn't had the presence of mind to phone Charles, things could have ended very badly for the entire Palmer family.

Once Ed had been picked up by the police, Lloyd decided to go into the office at the *Ledger* to see what the mood was among the other reporters. He also wanted to gauge whether or not he believed there was still a place for him at Houston's daily newspaper, or if he should move on to greener pastures.

When Lloyd walked into the news room, a hush engulfed the room, and his co-workers immediately stopped what they were doing. Applause burst forth suddenly, and the staff members gave him a standing ovation.

"Lloyd, we're so glad to see you in one piece," said one reporter, giving him a pat on the back and a handshake.

"I can't believe Ed would go so far," said another, "but thank God you're okay."

The comments by the others were along a similar vein, and Lloyd was genuinely overwhelmed and touched by the well wishers' sentiments. He had not been sure exactly what to expect when he arrived and was pleasantly surprised.

He went to his desk and performed the usual tasks — checking e-mails and voice mail messages, reviewing the *Ledger* web site for the most recently posted stories and searching the Internet for other news, both locally and nationally. After he had been there about thirty minutes, his phone rang. It was a call from within the *Ledger* offices, and the caller ID showed that Wilson Cox, the Ledger's executive vice president, was on the line.

"Lloyd Palmer here."

"Lloyd, this is Wilson Cox. Would you mind coming to my office right away, please?"

"No problem, Mr. Cox. I'll be right there," said Lloyd, and he hung up the phone. *This is it,* he thought. Cox had never summoned Lloyd to his office before, so he knew that, however the conversation went, it definitely would not be routine.

With all of the drama that had surrounded him during the past month, it was possible that the *Ledger* wanted to quietly sever their ties with him. If so, Lloyd planned to hold out for as much money as he could get— enough of a severance package so that he could take his time weighing his options.

Cox's office was on the building's top floor. Lloyd got off the elevator and approached the receptionist, who appeared to recognize him because she immediately said, "Mr. Cox is waiting for you in his office, Mr. Palmer. You can go right in." She pointed to the wooden door about ten feet away with a gold-plated sign bearing Cox's name. Lloyd knocked on the door and awaited a response.

"Come in," Cox said cheerfully, as Lloyd entered the office. Another elderly gentleman was seated in the chair closest to the window, but Lloyd did not recognize him. "I was just sitting here with Richard Nelson, and we were talking about you."

Lloyd sat in the chair closest to the door. "About me? Well, what's the verdict?"

"The verdict, Lloyd, is that you have literally saved our asses, not once but twice within a short period of time. If it hadn't been for you, the *Ledger* would have had a web of legal entanglements that we might not have survived. The fact that your life was in imminent danger is a source of shame and embarrassment as well. This paper owes you a tremendous debt, and we've thought of a great way to repay you."

"I didn't do the things I did because I expected to be repaid; I did them because they were the right things to do," responded Lloyd. "But I am curious as to what sort of payment you had in mind?"

"We want to offer you the position of editor of the paper. With Ed gone, the position needs to be filled right away. With the judgment you've shown and your ability to get the most out of a story and the players involved, you're the perfect candidate. We'll provide you with a salary and benefits package that is among the most competitive in the news business. How about it, Lloyd?"

This was not what Lloyd had expected, and he was stunned into silence. This would definitely be a groundbreaking move, but did he really want the pressure of being editor with the newspaper industry in such a state of flux?

"Your offer is very flattering. I'd like to have a day or so to think it over and talk to my wife, Stephanie, about it, if you don't mind."

"No, not at all. Take a day or think it over. But don't contemplate too long. We will need to fill the position soon. I'm sure you agree that Ed's arrest looks very bad for the paper, and we need someone to take charge immediately and put out the ensuing fires that will flare up until he's been sentenced, and the public forgets about what he's done."

"Don't worry. I should have an answer for you within the next couple of days," said Lloyd, as he felt his cell phone vibrate indicating that either a text message or a call was coming in. He stood up and shook both men's hands. "I'll let you two get back to your meeting."

Lloyd exited the office and closed the door. He checked his cell phone and it was a text message from Hamisi. *Meet me in 30 minutes at the place where we met before. Be sure to come alone.*

Lloyd had planned to go back to his desk and wait for incoming news for a fresh assignment, but then he remembered that Ed wasn't there, and he wasn't sure who was farming out stories that day. Instead, he told Charles to cover for him and headed to the Galleria area. He thought Hamisi had disappeared for good, and he wanted to speak to him once more before he vanished forever.

CHAPTER 54

Lloyd arrived at the Lakes on Post Oak about twenty-five minutes after receiving Hamisi's text message. It was a beautiful day; not a cloud in the sky. He sat on the same bench as before, awaiting Hamisi's quiet arrival. He didn't expect to hear his footsteps behind him. But, by now, Lloyd was accustomed to Hamisi's mysterious ways. In fact, he appreciated the precision of the cloak and dagger tactics.

He had been there about ten minutes when Hamisi's voice broke the silence. "I'm glad to see you in good health and unharmed."

Lloyd turned around to face his old friend. "Hamisi, I'm so glad to see you. I wasn't sure if I'd ever see you again. Why did you say you're glad to see me unharmed?"

"Our people took care of the man who was going to dismantle your car, did we not?"

"Your people? You mean that the Lemba had something to do with his broken neck?"

"Yes, our people were watching you because we felt that you might be in danger. Anyone who starts to peel away layers of deceit, the way one would peel away the layers of an onion, will ultimately become a target for those who do not want the truth to be revealed."

"Who are these people, Hamisi? You seem like you're a little mature to be engaging in hand to hand combat."

"We have a group among us that handles these sorts of missions. They carry no weapons, but their defense techniques are extremely effective."

"Professor Gastalt told me about an enforcement squad for the Lemba, but he said he had no proof of its existence. I want to thank you because you probably saved my life and the lives of my wife and daughter. I owe you so much, Hamisi. How can I ever repay you?"

"No payment is necessary. I do this because I have begun to look upon you as my own son. Your mind has been opened now, and you can see so many things you could not see before. This is what a parent does for a child — teaches him what he must know to become his best self."

"I have some interesting news, Hamisi. The *Ledger* has offered me the position of editor."

"So now you may be in a position to decide what is truth and what is not truth. What the people should know and what should be withheld from their consciousness. Will you take the job?"

"I really don't know, Hamisi. On the one hand, it could be a tremendous opportunity to make some changes in the way we report news. But I'll be up against a tremendous tide of a rapid race to the bottom. News standards have become increasingly lower, and the competition to report sleaze will only grow. I want to talk it over with Stephanie and then sleep on it for at least one night," Lloyd said, as he looked off into the distance.

"What about you? Where are you headed? Will you return to Houston any time soon?"

"I'm considering returning to Zimbabwe, but I haven't yet decided. The longer I stay in America, the more uncomfortable I am with the culture. A man must be who he really is or his inner light will dim and eventually go out."

"I think I understand what you mean. I just hope I will see you again someday."

"I hope so too, Lloyd. But, until then, you'll know that you're not alone. We consider you to be one of us now — an honorary Lemba. We'll always be watching."

The two embraced in a man hug. "I'll wait here until you're gone, like you asked me to before," said Lloyd, and he turned toward the lake, watching the ducks and swans glide across the water. He sat there for a couple of minutes, turned around, and Hamisi was gone.

--THE END--

AUTHOR'S NOTE

In 1999, I read a story in the *New York Times* about the Lemba tribe, a black tribe in southern Africa which could trace its origins back to Moses' brother Aaron through DNA markers. Because of its Biblical significance, particularly as it relates to African Americans, I had hoped that, as a result of the *New York Times* article, the origins of the Lemba would begin to receive wide exposure. Unfortunately, I have seen little to nothing in the media about the tribe since that time.

I have been a writer for many years and have published one non-fiction book but, until now, have never tried my hand at fiction. But I couldn't get the story about the Lemba tribe out of my mind, even years later. I thought a mystery which incorporated some of the history and traditions of the Lemba would give people a look into their lives and, perhaps, pique some newfound curiosity. I hope this book, *The Genesis Files*, will fulfill that purpose, as well as entertain, engage and inform.

I gleaned most of the information about the Lemba utilizing Internet research. The book titled, *Journey to the Vanished City: The Search for a Lost Tribe of Israel* by Tudor Parfitt, originally published in 1993, was also a useful reference regarding the history of the tribe. Parfitt, a historian, spent several months with the Lemba tribe in the 1980s while traveling throughout Southern Africa.

While this story is fictional, the history and most of the details about the Lemba tribe are factual. I decided to use a newspaper reporter as a vehicle for probing the details about the tribe and bringing some of the information to light and created the character Lloyd Palmer for that purpose. In addition, most of the incidents about which Lloyd reports are based on actual occurrences—either news stories that were reported in Houston media or situations that I personally witnessed. The names of the victims or perpetrators have been changed to protect their identities. Some of the details have also been changed and/or embellished for literary purposes.

I hope you enjoyed reading this story, and I appreciate comments and feedback. I can be reached via email at: **gwenrichardson@yahoo.com**.

Gwen Richardson

Houston, Texas

ORDER COPIES OF *THE GENESIS FILES*

Copies of this book can be ordered for $15.00 each (plus $5.00 for shipping and handling) through the following source:

> Cushcity.com
> 14300 Cornerstone Village Dr., Suite 370
> Houston, TX 77014
> Toll-free: 1-800-340-5454
> In Houston: (281) 444-4265

38454268R00174

Made in the USA
Columbia, SC
05 December 2018